A WARRIOR TO LOVE

JM MADDEN

I would like to thank my fantastic readers for going on so many journeys with me, and trusting me to give you a beautiful romance. I hope you love Booker and Catalina!

Thank you Mayas and Pamela for the Love Vixen submissions. They were perfect! And thank you to the other girls that submitted!

Sandie, as always, thank you for being you!

1

"Yes!" I hissed, watching the water swirl in the toilet, inches deeper than it should be.

It wasn't the normal response to an almost over-flowing toilet, but I now had a legitimate reason to call for help from the building manager, the elusive, hotter than hot, no-first-name Booker. Virginia didn't know what his first name was either, which was odd. Normally she knew everything about the residents of the building, because she'd lived here at the Willows the longest. Going on twenty years, supposedly. Virginia had created enough work for him that she should have known his full name by now, at the very least.

This day had just been...special. And not in the exceptional surprise-birthday-gift kind of special. No, special as in, I couldn't find one of my regular tennis shoes, a hair-tie had snapped my fingers when it broke going over my huge ponytail and my sister Francesca had shown up unexpectedly, Christopher in tow, and expected me to watch him. Since I worked from home, no one considered what I did a real job. 'Oh, you're just on the computer all day...'

So, for all that strife, I deserved to see tall, brooding Mr.

Booker today, with his sleek, close trimmed beard and mustache, and his penetrating green eyes. If he gave me more than a glance in the hallway, I think I would just drop my panties for him. The man was striking and unique. And I really hoped he was just as smart as he was pretty. Virginia seemed to think so. She kept extolling the man's virtues like he was about to go up for auction.

I didn't have time for fresh action. Normally, Chris, my nephew, was a doll-baby, but I was under contract and my deadline was looming, so I had worked while he'd played. I should have known the little bugger had been up to something, but he'd been so good all day. And he was so stinking cute. I probably wouldn't have yelled at him even if I'd spotted him flushing whatever he'd flushed.

"That's what I get for trusting a four-year-old," I muttered with a sigh.

Returning to the living room, I continued picking up the mess left in his wake, one ear cocked to the phone. Booker would be calling me back soon, hopefully. Maybe. Actually, did he ever return a call? Usually he just turned up in all his silent hotness, looking rugged and forbidding in his Levi's, boots and T-shirt. And the job today... how mortifying. At least it wasn't a tampon clogging the toilet. I'd learned that lesson a long time ago when Papa had talked to my sister and me after an expensive plumber call.

What was that thing called? A snake? I really hoped he had one of those things, because a plunger hadn't even budged the water level in the toilet. I had no idea what Chris had flushed, but it was lodged tight.

Thank goodness I even had a damn plunger. I'd only been here a few months and it seemed like I was continuously finding things I needed. It was hard being on my own. Evie had been the one to organize and stock and keep us on track. We'd grown up together in the burbs of Hilliard, Ohio and she'd been my best friend for as long as I could remember. Deliberate, calm, organized, Evie was an incredible person. She'd made her Barbies perch on the dresser in organized rows, their hair braided exactly the same. Her budgets had been just as tidy.

So, when we each got a job in the middle of the city, it seemed like a no-brainer to get an apartment together and split the costs. We'd had so much fun, going out on the weekends and enjoying the festivals Columbus put on every year. Then her company expanded and she'd moved up, until they'd offered her a job she couldn't refuse. In the middle of a literal jungle. I hadn't talked to her for weeks.

I hated the ache in my chest. It eased a little when we managed a text or a call, but she was so far away. Guyana was literally thousands of miles away, and a complete opposite time zone. The only thing that made the ache better was knowing that Evie was doing what she loved— teaching.

I'd been at the point in my career that my after-hours work was bringing in more money that my regular job, so I'd quit my job, packed up my stuff and found an apartment that spoke to me, on the Northside. The Willows was an older brick building, but it had character, and the current owners had renovated it, so everything was up to date. The change helped deal with Evie leaving.

Moving around the apartment, I picked up toys and returned things to their spots. It was almost in order when someone knocked on my door. Finally.

Crossing the room, my heart beating a little hard, I straightened my plain aqua-colored tee over my hips and tightened my abdomen. Not that it did anything. My curves were permanently curved and nothing was going to change it. Readying a smile, I swung the door open, looking for the tall, quiet, bearded form of the building manager.

Instead, it was the furry-faced, flat-footed, cheating mother pucker that used to be my ex-boyfriend. Anger surged in me. "What the hell are you doing here, Sean?"

I braced my bare foot-the one I hadn't yet found the shoe for-behind the door edge. The man was not coming into my space, damn it.

"Hey, baby," he moved forward expectantly and I leaned back out of lip reach. The guy was like a damn octopus and I wasn't putting up with it anymore. The bat that normally rested just beneath the door table to the left was on top of the entertainment center. I hadn't wanted Chris to get into trouble with it. "What do you want, you cheating asshole?"

A glimmer of anger darkened his crap-brown eyes. "I told you, baby, it didn't mean anything. She was just a waitress that was supposed to show me a good time. It was Vegas, baby, and you weren't supposed to know anything about it."

I gaped, my mouth moving as I sought words. "So, because it was in Vegas you didn't think it would matter to me?"

The absolute and utter gall of this man. Why had I put up with him for so long?

Sean rolled his eyes like he was running out of patience, but I didn't care. He was the one in the wrong, not me. "Get off my property, Sean. We're done, I've told you that too many times. We were done before the Vegas thing. Don't make me call the police."

His face darkened with fury and I realized that may not have been the best thing to say. Sean Holoman had had more than his fair share of run-ins with the cops, and he bashed them all the time. It was disturbing, some of the things he'd said, and that should have warned me a long time ago that he wasn't a stable individual. I glanced behind me, looking for a way to wedge the door shut, but there was nothing. I hadn't been prepared for this.

"Open the door, Cat, so we can talk about this," he wheedled. "You know you missed me."

"Leave, Sean. We're done. I told you that weeks ago."

"I let you have your little snit, but it's time to be done with it." He began to push against the door and I panicked. Where the hell was my phone? I need to call the cops.

"Open the door, Cat," he growled, pushing harder.

My feet began to slide on the carpet, and my pulse raced. "No!" I cried, leaning harder, straining.

One of his hands had wrapped around the edge of the door. Keys flew as I grabbed the bowl beside the door and tried to smash his hand. I landed two good hits to his fingers before he snatched them back, the door slamming shut. Panting, I twisted the dead-bolt home, tears filling my eyes when I realized what had just happened. I really needed to call the cops.

"Cat! Open the fucking door!"

I scanned my living room, looking for my phone. Where was it? Kitchen? I darted through the living room and scanned the kitchen. I'd just picked up my phone and flipped open the cover when Sean kicked the door open.

Terrified, my fingers fumbled as I keyed in my code and ran for the bedroom. I had just a glimpse of Sean's furious face as he focused on me, before I turned to look where I was going. Where could I go where he couldn't kick the door open? The front door was supposed to be the strongest, and it had been deadbolted!

I ran as fast as I could down the hall and toward my bedroom. It had two doors, though, and I knew before I got there he would catch me. Trying to think ahead, I slid to a stop and backtracked, heading for the front door. But Sean was faster than I was. I heard his booted feet slamming down the hallway behind me and I screamed, praying someone would hear me. It was the middle of the day, though, and everyone normal was at work. Virginia would never hear me. Her apartment was three floors down.

I switched gears again and lunged toward the entertainment center, and my trusty bat. It was a Louisville slugger Papa had given me and I knew it would make a dent in his damn head if I could grab it.

My T-shirt tightened across my chest and I twisted out of his grip, snatching the bat from the top of the entertainment center. Without even looking I swung it one-handed, feeling it clip something, then I lunged for the door again, but my bare foot was caught and I went down. "No! Let me go!"

I fell against the couch, bounced off and landed against the coffee table. Before I could even scream, he was on top of me, blood dripping down his chin where I must have clipped him. There was a snarl of pain on his face, and I'd never seen him look that vicious before. I couldn't ever remember seeing him in any kind of pain. His hands gripped my wrists.

"You fucking bitch. I ought to just strangle you now. I can't believe you hit me with a bat."

"You broke through my door, asshole. What did you expect?"

He gave me a smirk, leaning out enough that his chin dripped over my shoulder and not on my face. "I expect you to behave like a woman should and spread your legs."

Before I could think, he shoved one of his knees between mine, wedging them apart. Terror made me gasp in fear, and it was infuriating being unable to stop him, but he was strong. His family owned a construction business and he'd grown up working construction sites. I struggled harder than I ever had before. Impotent tears flooded my eyes, making it even harder to see, but I didn't know how to get out of this. "Let me go!" I screamed.

Sean shifted both of my wrists into one hand and slapped

me across the face. Pain consumed me and I was in shock. No one had ever struck me, not ever. Not even my parents.

If he was willing to hit me, he was willing to do more. I struggled until I couldn't breathe, my left cheek throbbing where he'd struck me. "Get...off...asshole!"

Then, suddenly, his suffocating weight was gone and he was flying backward through the air. I gasped in air. Booker leaned over me, his beautiful face hard with anger. "Are you okay?"

I nodded, my chest pounding, and took the hand he offered. Movement over his shoulder caught my attention. "Watch out!"

Booker turned, smoothly taking the tackle and spinning Sean away. It had looked so easy. Then Sean charged him again and Booker shifted, getting behind him. He put Sean in a head-lock and since Booker was so big, at least 6'3", he already had leverage on Sean. The smaller man was dancing on his toes, struggling, his face purple with fury as he beat at Booker's huge, implacable hands.

Booker looked directly at me, unconcerned with the man struggling in his grip. Muscles bulged in his chest and arms, but he seemed comfortable and in control. "Are you sure you're okay?"

I nodded, pushing my curly hair out of my face. It had come down at some point, and there was a tenderness on my scalp. Had he grabbed my ponytail? He must have.

I looked at my apartment. It was a wreck, and I didn't see my phone anywhere. The police needed to be called. Sean would go to jail for this and I didn't care what the fuck his issues with the police were.

The men began to struggle again. Sean slammed his fist down, I think hoping to get Booker in the balls, but he shifted and the hit landed on Booker's thigh. I could see Booker's arm tighten around Sean's neck. Then, suddenly, Sean was swinging his other hand down and I saw the glint of metal.

"Knife," I cried, but Booker had already seen it. He struggled to grab the arm that had the knife, but Sean was wily. He wrenched out of Booker's hold and spun, the knife swinging in an arc. It was terrifying, because my living room was not that big. As if hearing my thoughts, the knife slid through the back of my stuffed chair, the sound of fabric ripping loud over the exhalations of the men.

The thought of Booker being hurt terrified me.

Booker stopped moving and just stared at Sean, as if the guy was the most ridiculous thing he'd ever seen. "You need to drop the knife."

"Fuck you," Sean said, lunging.

Booker stepped casually to the side and Sean completely missed him, but he swung his arm backwards in a reckless swipe, and it hit. I gasped as Sean sliced through Booker's T-shirt and I prayed it didn't hit skin. Seconds later, I knew it had. Blood appeared on his abdomen, chilling me. Oh, shit.

Then something weird happened. Sean kicked out at Booker's legs, and something clunked. Sean jerked back, his foot obviously hurting. "You son of a bitch. What is that?"

I scrambled for the phone again and spied it in the crack of the couch cushions. Flipping the case open, I frantically tapped in my access code, but of course it was wrong. I couldn't control my shaking fingers. I glanced at the men.

Booker, still looking calm, was simply walking toward Sean, even though the other man still held the knife. Sean lunged again and this time, Booker swatted his hand away as if Sean were a child, then wrenched the man's arm behind his back. The knife fell to the floor, but Sean twisted in Booker's grip, one fist hitting Booker in the left temple. Booker staggered, blinking, and Sean followed it up with another punch to his face. I'd never seen Sean fight, but this was dirty.

Where was the damn bat? Miraculously, it was just a few

inches away, so I grabbed it up and lurched toward them. Before Sean could even look up, I swung the bat, hitting him hard in the back, which was to me. He cried out and when he turned, I sent the bat swinging into his gut. Gasping, he staggered, and it gave Booker enough time to plant a huge fist into Sean's jaw. He stiffened, blinked and fell over like a tree.

For a minute we both stared at the body sprawled on my living room floor. Was he really out?

I was surprised when broad hands gently took the bat from me. I hadn't even seen Booker move. "I think we're done with this," he said, voice rougher than normal.

I glanced up at him, standing over me. The guy was like a foot taller than I was, and probably a hundred pounds heavier. Blood covered the front of his shirt and there was a trickle flowing from the corner of his eye.

I needed to move. But I didn't know what to do. "Should we tie him up or something? He needs to go to jail."

Booker was staring at my mouth, and he shook his head. "No, we shouldn't tie him. Find your phone and call the cops. I'll watch him."

I retrieved my dropped phone and finally managed to get the right digits in. The calm voice of the 911 dispatcher almost made me cry, and she promised they would dispatch police immediately.

"And the EMTs," I told her. "My building manager has been hurt."

"Will do, ma'am."

Dropping the phone to the table, I hurried into the bathroom and retrieved a couple of clean towels from the cupboard. When I returned, Booker was leaning against the back of the chair that had been cut, looking pale. He also seemed to be leaning to the left, his right leg cocked oddly.

"Are you okay?" I asked. "Lift your shirt, please."

He turned his head to look at me and blinked, but his expression seemed a little dazed. For a moment, I stared, because his eyes were the truest green I'd ever seen on a person, and they were absolutely beautiful. He didn't seem to be tracking, though. I reached out and touched his forearm, resting on the chair, and he blinked, his expression clearing a little.

"Are you okay?"

He nodded his head, but I wasn't really sure about him. Something seemed off. I motioned to his shirt. "Can I look?"

There was no response as I reached for the hem of his T-shirt, sodden with blood. I lifted it up and held onto my control with a death grip, because it looked bad. I wasn't a person that enjoyed dealing with blood, but I could do it. Rolling one of the towels in my hands, I pressed it to the open gash. It seemed to have just barely skimmed along his muscles, but it hadn't gone deeper. Thank goodness!

There was blood coming from somewhere else, though, too. I looked my hero over from head to toe, and found another gash on his hand. This one was much deeper. He must have gotten it when he took the knife from him. It had been so fast I hadn't even seen the knife connect. I rolled another towel and wrapped his hand around it. "Hold this, tight."

Then I made sure the towel across his belly was tight. I tried to get him to sit down, but he wouldn't do it. So, I held that towel the entire time we stood there, waiting for the cops and the ambulance to arrive. I tried to talk to Booker, but he seemed intent on staring at Sean, making sure he didn't move. And when the police arrived, tromping down the hallway, I called out to let them know we were okay and that the assailant was on the floor.

A male officer, looking experienced and maybe a little bored, asked me to explain what had gone on. I replayed everything as clearly and concisely as I could. I had never dealt with cops, though, and I fumbled a few times, nervousness twisting my syllables. I didn't want them to think that I had invited Sean over, so I told them that, several times, and that I thought I was going to be beaten and raped.

The tears came, then, surprising me, because I considered myself kind of a badass. Today had shown me how far off the mark I was. Booker, finally appearing more aware, wrapped an arm around my shoulders. "You did good, Catalina."

I sagged into him just for a tiny moment, feeling his strong arms wrap around me. The towel stayed firm, though. I wouldn't let him bleed to death.

The other two policemen had been prodding Sean, trying to get him to wake up. Finally, he started coming around, and he was not happy. When he looked up and saw the cops standing over him, he went still like a frantic horse, then went ballistic. Within seconds he was up off the floor and trying to run out the door. For the second time that day, I saw him taken to the ground. The cops had cuffs, though, and they slapped them on him quicker than shit.

Sean started yelling as soon as they started fighting, and he didn't stop the entire time they fought to cuff him. Then he caught sight of Booker and me, standing together.

"You're going to pay for this, bitch. I swear to you."

The cops wrestled him out the door and down the hallway, but he screamed the entire time. It was terrifying and chilling, and so out of the normal for me. I led a fairly mundane life, dreaming up ideas for other people. This kind of stuff didn't happen to me.

The ambulance people arrived then, carrying bulging emergency bags and pushing a gurney. They came straight for Booker, encouraging him to sit on the gurney. One of them gently pulled my hand away from Booker's abdomen, checking the damage.

"I think this will be fine, ma'am. Looks like you got the bleeding mostly stopped."

I sagged with relief. I'd actually done something right today. I looked at Booker, watching as they checked his vitals.

"I think you might have a concussion," one of the medics told Booker, using a penlight to shine in his eyes. Then he moved to his hand, gently unrolling his fingers. Pulling the towel away, he quickly replaced it with gauze when it started bleeding again. "You'll need stitches in this, as well. Anything else we need to know about?"

Booker frowned. "I have a history of TBI."

The mood changed, subtly, at his words. The paramedics grew more focused.

"Wait, what's TBI?" I asked.

"Traumatic brain injury," one of the men said without looking at her. "You know you have to go in, then."

Booker grimaced. "I know."

"If it makes you feel any better, you'll probably need a few stitches anyway," one of them said with a smile.

Booker's lips quirked beneath his dark mustache, but no more.

"I'm so sorry," I told him, really and truly meaning it. I wanted to cry at the damage that had been done to him. The man was so handsome, it was a crime that he'd been damaged this way.

"Not your fault," he said, voice more gruff than normal. "Might have to fix your toilet later."

I laughed, though it came out kind of teary. "I can wait. I'll come to the hospital in a little bit. Can I bring you anything?"

Booker grimaced, but it might have been because they were bandaging his hand. "No, I'll be fine."

I watched as they wheeled him out of my tiny apartment. This day had gone in the crapper, in more ways than one.

Growling in pain, I tried not to bitch at the intern doing the stitches, but she was not doing a good job. Even with the local, I could feel every stitch she made.

Then she got to an especially deep spot and I grabbed her hand before I could stop myself. The woman looked up in fear, then blushed tomato red. "If the patient can feel the pain you need to administer more local," I told her, trying not to treat her like she was stupid.

The young woman nodded, going pale, and I let her go. She spun to the rolling cart and loaded up a syringe of medicine. An older woman stuck her head into the bay through the curtain. "How's he doing?"

"He's feeling pain, so I'm administering more local."

The older woman nodded. "Good girl," she said, and disappeared.

I smirked. The medical system was so messed up. Why wasn't the resident in here watching the intern? Guiding her? Last I heard they were making plans to take me for a CT scan, but I didn't think I needed it. I hadn't passed out or vomited, like with some concussions I'd had, even though the asshole had hit me in a particularly sensitive spot. I'd had my skull cracked there once by the butt of a rifle, and headaches moved in almost exclusively on that left side, then radiated outward.

Yeah, the guy's fist had rung my bell, definitely, but there would be no lasting effects. No more than there already were, anyway. So far they'd missed the hearing loss on that side and I, certainly, would not tell them about it. It had happened a long time ago and what happened today didn't affect it one way or the other. Now, if the fucker had hit my other ear, it might have been a different kind of conversation.

Voices yelled outside the curtain. I cocked my head to try to figure out what was going on. I heard a distinctive, 'ma'am, you can't do that,' and the curtain to the cubicle was ripped back. Catalina stood there in all her beautiful glory, her eyes wide and her mouth tight with anger. Her long, dark curls seemed especially wild and mussed tonight, but maybe that had been from the fight earlier. There were lines of black makeup down her face and her left cheek was red and swollen, but I didn't think she'd ever looked more beautiful.

Catalina Rivera was my... hell, I didn't know what she was, other than an enormous distraction. I tried to do my job, but if she was in the area, she shot my concentration to hell. The woman was beautiful and, as she'd proven tonight, a huge load of drama.

That wasn't really fair. From what I'd seen, she'd had no choice in what had happened today.

"You can't be in here, ma'am," the harried clerk said, reaching for Catalina's arm.

She'd been grabbed too much today and my anger spiked again. "Get your hands off her."

The woman released Catalina. "She still can't be in here if she's not family. She needs to wait outside like everyone else."

"She's my fiancée and I want her here," I snapped, glowering at the woman. "Go bug someone else."

"But, she..."

"Fuck off, lady," I said, tired of dealing with her.

Catalina's mouth fell open, and I replayed what I'd said. Oh, yeah, the fiancée part. What the hell had I been thinking? There was supposed to be no interaction between us.

Catalina was rightfully shocked, and maybe not in a good way. She blinked at me several times, her cinnamon-colored eyes wide in her pale face, and her plump lips working just a little. Then the attitude rolled in and she tried to look down at the woman, though she wasn't much more than five feet tall.

It worked though, because the attendant/guard dog turned with a huff and slammed the curtain shut behind her.

Catalina grinned at him and stepped closer to see what the intern was doing. "Oh, your pretty abs..." she breathed, and jerked like she'd just realized she'd said it out loud.

I chuckled, though it hurt my pretty abs to do it. It had hurt to sit up and yell at the woman too, but I wasn't going to watch Cat take the woman's aggravation.

Cat? When had I started thinking of her like that?

She stopped beside the gurney, and there were tears in her eyes. I tried to reach out, but she was a little too far away. "I'm okay," I told her. My voice sounded especially gruff, tonight, and I wondered if she even understood what I said.

The intern drew my attention back to what she was doing by tugging on one of the stitches as she tied it off. "You could have ripped these open doing that," she grumbled. "The doctor will be in shortly to look at your hand."

Yeah, that injury was a little more in-depth. I wouldn't have let the intern work on it even if she'd tried. It didn't feel like any of the tendons were hit, but I hadn't flexed it enough to be sure.

It burned like the blazes. I'm sure the knife the guy used had been super-clean, too.

After the intern left, I tried to read Catalina's face. Normally, she was almost irritatingly upbeat, smiling her broad, pretty smile at everyone. There was disillusionment in her expression today that I didn't like. "Are you okay?"

She blinked, her long lashes shading her cheeks as she looked down at her clasped hands. "I'm fine," she said, forcing a smile as she looked up at me again. "I'm just worried about you. What did they say about your hand?"

I sighed, knowing she wasn't telling me everything. I wasn't in a position to demand answers from her, though. "Oh, you know, looks like it got cut with a knife." I shrugged, trying not to look too worried. "They have a plastic surgeon coming in to stitch it up. One cut is close to some nerves."

Catalina made a face and her eyes filled with tears. Shit, I shouldn't have said anything. "Hey," I said, reaching out to pinch her shirt-sleeve and draw her close. "It's all good. Really."

She shook her head, wiping her eyes. "It's not, though. You were really hurt. I can't believe I got taken in by him. He seemed so nice, at first. Then he went complete, full-on asshole."

I sighed, not sure what to say to her. Not all guys were assholes. I could *behave* like an asshole, but that was different. I didn't think she was able to understand the difference, at least not today. "Not all guys are assholes."

She looked up at me, her big, soft brown eyes swimming in tears, and I wanted to kiss her. I'd wanted to kiss her ever since I'd moved into the building. That was why I'd made myself stay away from her. I only went to her apartment if there was something seriously wrong and she'd called, which meant I couldn't avoid her. Just being in the same building was usually close enough.

"Did you know he was coming when you called me?"

"Absolutely not," she said, her eyes going wide. "I broke up with him weeks ago because he cheated, but he thinks he's charming enough to win me back. He's obviously not. I filed the police report before I came in here. Tomorrow I'll have to go request a protection order."

The sincerity was there on her face, so I believed her. It was a good thing I'd arrived when I did.

"I think that's smart," I told her. "He's going to be pissed when he gets out."

"Well, he decked a cop on the way to the cruiser, so I don't think he'll be getting out soon."

I snorted, then winced as my stomach quivered with pain. The numbing was wearing off. If I could get my damned hand done, I'd be on my way home.

The curtain swung open, then, and an older, well-groomed man entered. "Mr. Booker, I hear you got into a knife fight."

The doctor wheeled the rolling stool over to look at my handing hand, gently peeling the bandaging away. "This is going to hurt. I apologize."

Cat circled the gurney to my other side and reached out to hold my good hand. I blinked at her, not sure exactly what to do or say, but she just gave me a smile. If it made her feel better, who was I to argue?

3

I didn't like being in the room while Booker was stitched up, but I didn't feel safe leaving him alone. Or maybe I was the one that didn't want to be alone. Either way, I watched the plastic surgeon numb his hand, then plant a long row of little tiny stitches into his skin. The meat of his thumb required heavier stitches, but Booker never flinched. He watched the entire process, occasionally asking the surgeon why he did something.

The doctor wiped his hand down and wrapped it. "You need to keep this dry for the next two days. The stitches can come out in two weeks. Just make an appointment with my office. Baby it for the first few days, then you can start using it more. If anything doesn't feel right, make an appointment with my office."

Booker removed his hand long enough to salute him, then wrapped his fingers around mine again.

"I'll let them know I'm done and they'll find you a room."

"I'm not staying the night," Booker said.

The surgeon frowned at him. "Didn't the resident say something about a concussion and TBI?"

Booker shrugged his broad shoulders. "Doesn't matter. I'm not staying."

I watched the two of them, but didn't say anything. Booker should probably spend the night, but it wasn't my place to tell him that.

"I'll send your doctor in and you can talk to her about it."

Booker looked at me and I was struck with how strange the situation was. We barely knew each other, yet here I was, holding his hand and pretending to be his fiancée. We were presenting this united front that we really weren't, and I felt a little deceitful.

A tall, spare woman with dark hair I hadn't seen before stepped into the cubicle. "What's this I hear about you refusing to stay? You just had a major trauma. You need to be monitored overnight."

Booker's gaze hardened. "Not really. The knife wounds were superficial. The head trauma minimal. There was no loss of consciousness, so you're not even really justified in doing a CT scan. It won't show if I have a concussion, anyway. So, you're left with observing me. Which I don't want. I can go home and be more comfortable. If I need anything, I can come back in."

The woman glowered but seemed to agree with his statements. I hadn't known that about the concussion not showing up on the CT scan. Why had they been planning one, then?

"You'll have to go AMA," she said eventually.

"I understand," Booker said, sighing. "God forbid anyone hold you liable."

The doctor turned her hard gaze to me. "Are you staying with him?" she demanded.

I opened my mouth to respond, then just nodded. It was the least I could do. "I will. What do I need to watch for?"

"Loss of consciousness, extreme dizziness, vomiting.

Anything out of the ordinary. If any of that appears, bring him in immediately. Did someone check you out?"

"Yes, ma'am."

And they had. Nothing was broken, though, so they'd given me a Tylenol and an ice pack. Somewhere in the argument to find Booker, I'd lost the ice. It was probably why my head was throbbing now, and my eye was swelling shut. I must look like a damn horror movie extra.

Within half an hour, Booker was signing paperwork to leave and I was walking through the parking lot toward my car to return and pick him up. I fidgeted with my phone as I waited for him to appear at the emergency department door. I wasn't a nurse, obviously, and I worried about being responsible for him.

Then he appeared at the door, being wheeled by an orderly. The chair seemed too small for him. Though we'd been here for hours, he looked good, chestnut colored hair curling over his forehead. Well, except for the crazy cut and bloody shirt. He pushed up out of the chair as soon as the intern stopped, and staggered a little as he gained his balance, then he limped to the car.

As he settled into the car beside me, he tucked some papers between the chair and console. "Did you hurt your leg?" I asked.

"No. Old injury."

He cringed at the light of the setting sun coming through the windshield. The spring days were getting longer, now, and the sun was staying up longer. Saying nothing, I handed him my Ray Bans. He took them without a word and slipped them on. Anything had to be better than nothing.

Within twenty minutes we'd returned to the apartment building. It had been a silent ride home, but I thought he might have dozed a little. As soon as we pulled into the parking lot, he lifted his head and looked around. I got the feeling he was suddenly on alert, and I wondered about his background.

Virginia had said he'd been in the military, but that really didn't tell me anything. I so wanted to ask questions...

I pulled into my spot and parked. Before I could gather my bag and get out, he was already rolling out of the car. I could tell his stomach was hurting, because he walked a little hunched. And there was still something off about his walk. Had that kick damaged him, or something? I scrambled to open the front door of the building. When he started down the hallway toward his office and apartment, I don't think he even realized.

"Booker, you need to come to my place. I need to clean up and I can watch you better there."

He paused and turned. "I don't expect you to follow through with the promise you made the doctor. I'm fine, Catalina."

I moved to stand in front of him. "You're not fine. It's going to get harder for you to do things soon because the pain medication is wearing off. You need to just come up and chill at my place. I have food in the fridge and a recliner."

"I need to at least check on my dog, listen to my messages, and make sure there are no emergencies."

I tried not to roll my eyes. "Virginia knows you were injured. I'm sure the entire building knows that you were attacked. Wait, you have a dog?"

4

"Oh, my gosh," Catalina breathed. "He's incredible!"

Yeah, I got that reaction a lot. Blue was a full-blooded black and tan Doberman Pinscher, muscular and intimidating, his pale brown eyes focused completely on me and the intruder behind me. "His name is Blue."

I touched Catalina's shoulder. "Blue, she's okay. This is Cat."

If possible, the dog's attention sharpened even more, because I'd said one of his favorite words. Terrorizing the neighborhood strays was one of Blue's favorite things to do. He just liked the chase, though, he never hurt the cats.

Catalina held her hand out to the dog and I urged him forward. "It's okay, buddy."

"He's so beautiful! Doberman?"

"Yes. Blue is two years old and smarter than most humans I know."

Catalina barked out a laugh. "I don't doubt it. My brother-in-law had one, Zeus, and he was incredibly smart. Incredibly goofy, too, though," she laughed.

"Yeah, he has those moments as well."

The dog's sharply tipped ears quivered as he reached out to smell Catalina's hand. He seemed to accept that she wasn't a danger, but he wouldn't let her pet him. When Cat reached out, Blue drew back. Cat didn't push it, though, which impressed me.

The dog swiveled his focus to me and I could tell he wanted to greet me like the pup he was, but I held him off. I let him sniff the bandage on my hand and it seemed to worry him. "I'm okay, buddy."

I moved through the apartment to the antiquated answering machine. I'd tried to get the residents to use my cell-phone or just text, but most of them had been here so long that the original office number was the one they used. There were no messages. Huh.. That was odd. I usually had about three a day, some legit and others not so legit. I'd been gone for hours and no one had called.

I felt relieved. I could take some time out and not worry I was putting anyone off.

"No messages," I told Cat.

She nodded. "I called Virginia at the hospital and told her you weren't going to be available for at least a day. I'm sure she let everyone know."

Yes, that explained it.

Virginia was a lovely busybody with her finger on the pulse of the Willows. She knew everyone in the building and had more finesse in her little pinky than I could ever dream of having. More than once I'd walked away from her apartment wondering what the hell I'd agreed to.

Virginia had been one of the contributing factors in my fascination with Catalina. Every time I saw Virginia, she had a new Catalina anecdote. It drove me nuts, and yet I found myself hanging on her every word.

Virginia had told me we would be a good fit, but I didn't even want to think about that. Working at the Willows and taking care of my dog kept me busy enough. Besides, I wouldn't make anyone be with me the way I was.

My hand throbbed painfully and it felt like it was beginning to swell. I was supposed to elevate it, but I hadn't gotten that far.

"Let's head upstairs," Cat said, turning. "Blue is welcome to come."

"I...need a few minutes. Can I just meet you up there?"

Catalina cocked her head and glanced around. "I can wait. Do what you need to do."

Well, shit. "I'll be back in a few."

I hoped I wasn't lying to her. I walked through the back door of the office and into the apartment, then into the bedroom, unfastening my pants as I went. When Sean kicked me, he'd done something. I sat on the side of the bed and slipped my prosthetic off, turning it in my hand. I didn't know if one of the sensors had been jostled loose, or what...

I removed the access door on the microprocessor of the ankle joint and immediately saw the problem. One of the wires had popped off its mounting point inside. It might have even been loose before the altercation with Sean, then his kicking the joint had popped it off. Scrambling for the little tool kit on my dresser, I reattached the wire and refit the socket. I moved around the room, bending and flexing. It was perfect. That one little wire had prevented it from bending correctly, which had made me limp like a damn old man. I took a few minutes in the bathroom to wipe down, then changed my shirt. I'd love to just curl up on my bed, but Catalina was sitting on my couch waiting for me. I grabbed a pair of sleep pants to change into later and walked out to the living room.

"Ready?" Catalina asked, smiling at me as much as she could without hurting herself. She looked like she needed sleep as well. And another ice pack.

"He needs to go out first."

We stopped at the back courtyard and I let the dog out to do his thing. We were going to have to start cutting the grass soon. Blue went from bush to bush, watering as he went, but he returned fairly quickly, still keeping close to my thigh. Catalina wasn't threatening, but Blue would keep his distance until he was ready to be social.

"This is ridiculous," I complained, even though I knew it sounded whiny. "I don't really need to be watched. I've had concussions before and I know what to be on the lookout for."

Catalina blinked at me, her dark cinnamon-colored eyes huge in her pale face. "Yeah, unless you keel over, unconscious, and your pretty dog eats your face off."

I stopped and looked at her. She shrugged defensively, looking cute and rumpled. "It could happen. And then I would feel like shit for the rest of my life. Come on. You just have to spend one night and let me wake you up occasionally."

I huffed out a breath. "Fine."

Inside, I was kind of jumping up and down. This was the chance I'd been looking for, getting to know the woman without really committing to anything.

I smirked a little when I realized how much I'd fallen. In high school, I'd been the football quarterback. Attention had been showered on me like rain, and I'd sucked it up. Girls had come easy, scholarships had come easy, but I reached a point where it had been *too* easy, and I'd wanted more challenge. My friend's older brother had signed up for the military, and I'd been intrigued enough to go down to the recruiter's office and gather up an armload of material on the different branches. I could still remember flipping open the brochure for the Army Rangers and feeling like I'd found what I wanted to do.

And for the most part, being a Ranger had been easy too. Thanks to good genetics, I had a powerful machine, and the physical part had been just challenging enough to be interesting.

The injuries... well, they had been the hardest to deal with. Over the course of eight years of active duty, I'd had more injuries than I could even remember. So many concussions. I'd had three vehicles blown out from underneath me over the course of my career, more than a dozen broken bones, I had partial vision in one eye and complete hearing loss in the left ear. Three bullet holes. Oh, and a below the knee amputation that ached like a sonofabitch, even years after it was gone.

But hey, I was still moving. Which was more than a lot of my buddies.

I followed Cat onto the elevator, scrambling for something to talk about. It seemed very quiet and heavy, and I suddenly realized why. I was such an ass.

"Are you sure you want to go to your apartment? We can stay in mine."

Catalina shook her head, looking determined. "I need to get back in my space. He's not going to chase me out of it."

She almost seemed to reconsider when she pushed her door open. The entire door jamb had been broken. It was obvious she'd shut the dead-bolt trying to keep him out; it was still in the extended position. The jamb had just given way to the force of his boot. The boot print was on the door.

Inside, there were definite signs of a struggle. I watched Catalina's face, waiting for some kind of breakdown, but she kept it together. Stepping through the mess, I allowed her to direct me to the couch. "If you chill here for a few minutes, I'll get you a blanket and something to eat if you'd like."

The thought of food didn't appeal to me right then, but I let her putter around, putting her space back to rights. Blue sniffed the area directly around me, then stood at the end of the couch.

It would take a while for him to feel comfortable enough in the space to settle down.

I relaxed down into the couch and realized how tired and in pain I really was. My ribs ached from being punched and my head throbbed. As if sensing I was having issues, Cat crossed to the drapes on the far side of the room and closed them, blocking out the waning light. It had been after twelve when I'd climbed on the elevator to come up here to fix her toilet. Now it was evening. Allowing my body to tip over, I settled my head onto a plush pillow that smelled like her, and was out.

～

I WATCHED the big man shift in pain and finally relax on my couch. Tiptoeing to the hall closet, I retrieved a blanket from the dryer. It was fresh and soft and hopefully not too warm.

Eyeing the dog as I moved close, I tried to appear unthreatening as I prepared to throw something big and dark over his master. Luckily, the dog didn't move, and neither did Booker as I tugged the blanket up to his lightly bearded chin.

He'd relaxed in sleep and I took a minute to really look at him. His strong face was normally so closed down. Yes, he was definitely handsome, but there was a reserve to him that gave him a forbidding demeanor. Something about his eyes, or the set of his full mouth. I don't ever remember seeing him smile, or laugh, but then, I hadn't had a lot of contact with him. Maybe it was the light beard that made him look intimidating. It was more of a goatee with a line of hair along his jaw, and it was always perfectly trimmed.

Turning away from his long sprawl, I went back to picking up random items that had been knocked around. My cheek throbbed every time I bent over and I wondered if I shouldn't ice it again. Maybe I should, but I wasn't sure I had the energy to do it.

I boiled a cup of water in the microwave for tea. Should I wake Booker up to eat something? We'd both missed dinner, I was sure. I debated for a couple of minutes, then decided I'd give him an hour to nap, before warming something up for both of us. Dropping a tea bag in the cup, I retreated to my office in the second bedroom.

I loved my little work spot. I had an L-shaped desk in one corner. There was a window I could open or close, depending upon my mood and the sometimes crazy Ohio weather, and more storage than I knew what to do with. Sitting at the desk, I brought my computer to life, pulling up a client file. I'd lost a lot of work time today, and I needed to make it up.

At one point I felt like I was being watched. Swiveling my head, I saw Blue standing at the door, just looking at me. The dog was definitely intimidating, and he had to weigh at least a hundred pounds, but I didn't get any danger vibes from him. In a way, I appreciated him being here since the front door was completely useless. I'd propped a chair under the door handle, but that wasn't much of a deterrent.

Blue moved away from the doorway and I glanced at the clock. It was time to go check on Booker, anyway.

The guy was snoring, obviously deeply asleep, and I hated to wake him. Maybe I would get something ready for him to eat, then wake him up. I went into the kitchen and rummaged in the fridge. He seemed like a meat eater, so I defrosted some boneless chicken thighs. I could make a creamy mushroom garlic chicken over rice that was pretty damn good, so that's the direction I took. It wasn't specifically oriental, but if he wanted to flavor it with soy sauce, he could. Maybe I should go ahead and throw some egg rolls in the air fryer. What the hell.

Within twenty minutes I had a decent late dinner simmering, and I went into the living room to wake him up.

"Booker," I said softly, then louder. "Hey, do you think you can eat something?"

Blue gave a kind of woof and Booker jerked up on the couch, a hand going to his head. Blue moved in and snuffled at him. Booker rubbed the dog on the ears, then down his neck. "I'm okay, buddy."

"Dinner is about ready," I told him, and Booker jerked, looking up at me. Then he looked around the room, and I realized he had no idea where he was. "You're in my apartment," I told him softly. "You helped me out with my ex, remember? Kinda kicked his ass really nice."

I forced a smile, though I was worried that he didn't seem to recognize me. Then his expression and those brilliant green eyes cleared as his face relaxed. "Catalina. Sorry, I didn't remember where I was."

One arm wrapped around his middle and he hunched over like he was in pain. The couch probably wasn't a great place for him to rest. He needed to stretch out and be comfortable.

"Come in and sit at the breakfast counter. Or I can bring you a plate here."

Booker held up a hand and squinted up at me. "I'll come in."

I had cleared off the counter and set out two plates with silverware. "If you want to make a plate at the stove, you can eat here."

Without a word, he grabbed one of the plates and moved toward the food. He didn't take as much as I expected him to, and I wondered if he wasn't a little nauseous. Bad concussions could cause nausea. He dove into the food like he'd been denied meals, though, then went back for seconds. "This is really good," he told me at one point, then went back to eating.

"How is your head feeling?"

He glanced at me, his head cocked. "It's fine, really. I've been a lot more hurt than this."

"What branch of the military were you in?" I asked, wondering if he minded talking about it.

"Army Rangers. Deployed nine times." He shrugged, his shoulders a little hunched.

"Damn. I'm sorry."

"Don't be," he said quickly. "I was doing what I wanted to do."

Booker cleaned up his plate, then pushed it aside. "What more did they say about your...ex? I was kind of not firing on all cylinders when they took him away."

"I requested that they file charges and I have to go down to the courthouse tomorrow to apply for a protection order." The thought of doing that alone made my stomach twist, but I would do it. The asshole had kicked in my door and had hit me. And he'd hurt Booker. Who knows what he would have done if Booker hadn't rescued me.

Nobody should be able to get away with that kind of behavior.

"You won't see him, though, right?"

I shrugged. "I do not know. I've never had to do this before."

Booker nodded and reached out to scratch the dog, sitting at his knee. I waited to see if he would offer to go with me, but he didn't. I fought disappointment, then anger at myself. This was not his issue, it was mine, and I would deal with it however it needed to be done. With or without help.

"How long did you date him?" he asked, his voice gruff.

"Not very long," I sighed. "I was set up by a friend of a friend and he was nice at first. We went on a few dinners and did a hockey game. Then he had a supposed business convention in Vegas. I knew it was a boys' trip, but whatever. If you can't trust a guy you shouldn't be with him, you know? I had already decided to break up with him. There was no chemistry."

Booker gave me an odd look, but I wasn't sure why.

"We never even had sex," I blurted, then wondered why the hell I'd had to say it like that. The skin of my face grew hot. "So, he didn't technically cheat on me, I guess."

Oh, god, did he have a girlfriend? No... surely he would have said something if he did. He'd called me his fiancée at the hospital. Yes, I knew it was fake, but would he have done that if there was another woman in the wings? I would hope not.

"Anyway, I was breaking up with him before all this mess. Sean thinks he's God's gift to women, and I don't have the time to cater to that shit."

I laughed, and Booker's lips quirked. "I don't blame you."

I stood and began gathering dishes. Before I could take Booker's, he'd gotten to his feet and had walked it to the sink, setting the stoneware carefully inside. He moved gingerly and I wondered if the pain was returning. "The hospital sent some pain pills home with you. Want me to see if you can take one?"

"No. I don't like to take them any more than I have to. Whatever they gave me at the hospital nauseated me a little."

The dog moved to lean against his leg and he stroked the sleek black fur. He had long fingers, competent hands. Sean had been a strong beast, but Booker had been able to control him. The man was a hero to me.

"I haven't thanked you yet," I told him.

Booker scowled. "Don't thank me. I just happened to show up at the right time."

"Regardless, you helped me, and I appreciate it more than I can tell you. Whether you want it or not, you have my appreciation."

Something flared in his eyes, but he turned away, and I wondered what the emotion had been. Running the faucet hot, I rinsed the dishes, then put them in the dishwasher. Booker moved back to the counter and sat down, and I was very conscious of him behind me. At one point I looked up and he was staring at me, hard. I glanced away and I could feel the flush roll over the skin of my face. Hopefully, he wouldn't see how much his regard set me on edge. I scrambled for something to talk about.

"I think I would have been okay if my nephew hadn't been here today."

"Why do you say that?"

"Because I normally keep my baseball bat right by the door, but I had put it out of reach because Chris was coming over. He's also the reason for the toilet call."

Booker scrubbed a hand over his face. "I'll fix that now," he said, pushing to his feet.

"No, you won't," I told him, holding out a hand and stalling his movement. "I have two bathrooms for a reason. Anyway, that's not the point of the conversation. I don't like feeling like a woman in distress. That's not who I am."

He stared at me, not commenting. I shook my head, not sure where I was going with this. "It was just a series of actions that piled up into an emergency. And now I'm helping you out by making sure you wake up in the morning. Who would feed your dog if you didn't?"

His full lips quirked slightly, and I was glad I'd at least gotten that much. Booker leaned back in the chair and cocked an arm over the back. "I think he'd find a way to survive. Blue was chained in a yard as a guard dog when I stole him. He was just a pup."

I gaped, glancing at the dog again. "Seriously?"

Oh, damn. He was a hero to animals, too.

"The guy that owned him had gone to jail, so I felt safe

taking him from the yard. He'd just had his ears trimmed and they were dirty and infected. He latched onto me like a tick."

Snorting, I looked at Blue with new understanding. No wonder the dog doted on him the way he did. Booker rescued everyone, it seemed like.

"Did he ever get out of jail?"

Booker shrugged. "If he did I never heard about it. That was another state, anyway."

"Well, even if the dog is used to starving, we'll make sure that doesn't happen. I'll wake you a couple of times through the night, okay?"

"I suppose..." Booker said, frowning. Then he yawned, covering his mouth with his bandaged hand. It looked a little swollen.

"If you follow me, I'll show you where you can sleep tonight."

While he'd been resting on the couch and I'd been waiting on dinner to cook, I'd stripped my bed, replaced the sheets with fresh and picked up a few things. If he woke in the night, he'd be close to the bathroom and there was plenty of room to stretch out on my bed. Heck, the dog could sleep with him if he wanted to.

"I'm not taking your bed," he growled as he followed me into the room.

"Um, actually, you are." I moved to the bed and pulled back the comforter and sheet. "It's a heck of a lot better than the couch. You were all scrunched up on it. And there's plenty of room for the dog here too."

Booker looked like he wanted to argue, but I held up a hand. "As your fiancée," I grinned teasingly, "I'm going to insist. You need to go to bed."

One side of his mouth quirked up. "Are you joining me?"

The question took me off guard. Then a slow heat rolled

through my belly and I fought not to shudder. I had not expected that teasing, sly look. Should I respond?

"I don't feel like we know each other well enough yet," I laughed.

"We're about to," he warned, reaching for the button of his jeans.

For a minute I wanted to just stand there and watch him strip, but he deserved privacy. Unless he needed help... "Are you okay here?"

The man lifted a brow at me teasingly, and I'm sure I blushed furiously before I spun away to stalk out of the room. I would check on him in a little while.

5

Twice that night I was woken by an angel in flannel sitting at the edge of the bed.

The first time Catalina woke me, I could barely open my eyes. Had to be because the pain meds were still wearing off. She gave me a bottle of water and asked me if I wanted more pain medication. I'm not even sure I answered her.

The second time she woke me, I roused more fully. The cut in my hand throbbed with every heartbeat, and I propped it against the headboard. "What time is it?"

"Like, three," she whispered, voice husky. "A little after."

In the light from the bathroom she looked bleary-eyed, but incredibly sexy, with her thick dark hair over one shoulder. Without even pausing to consider how forward it was, I reached out and felt her hair. It was silky and soft. The curl flattened with my touch, then tightened again when I released it. "You have a lot of hair," I murmured.

She chuckled lightly. "I do. It's been the pride and the bane of my existence my entire life."

"I bet."

"Do you need pain pills?"

My hand was in agony and my stomach was aching. Surprisingly, my head hurt the least. "Maybe just a couple of ibuprofen. Not the hospital stuff."

"Okay," she said quickly, and disappeared into the bathroom. Moments later, she returned with three small brown pills in her hand, and I realized how much my gut ached, but I took the pills and swallowed them down, then swung my legs off the bed, sitting beside her. Catalina slapped a hand to her mouth and stared. Oh, yeah.

"Sorry. You didn't know I was an amputee?"

"No, I fucking didn't know you were an amputee," she gasped. "When would I have learned that?"

I sighed, wishing that it could just be done. I hated when people made a big deal over it. Especially women. God, some of the looks I'd gotten... On top of everything else that had happened today, though, it probably was pretty shocking to Catalina. "I'm sorry you didn't know. I guess I could have told you at the hospital, but it was already an uphill battle to get out of there."

"Yeah, I get that. I'm sorry I reacted so harshly. Did Sean damage your prosthetic earlier?"

"Just a little," I told her. "I reattached the wire and it's good as new. "

"Okay, good. And your head?" she asked softly.

"Not bad. I've had worse concussions. I told you that. It doesn't bother me nearly as much as my hand."

I flexed the fingers. They felt swollen, like sausages. I'm just glad it wasn't my dominant hand. Catalina took my hand in her own, resting it in her lap as she peered down and peeked beneath the bandage. "Do you think we should ice it or something?"

I stared down at her bent head, at a loss. When was the last time anyone had worried over me, or my health? My parents asked after me, but it was more of a social nicety than actual concern. They were done raising me and let me live my life, even though they didn't approve of it. Once I'd tossed away the college scholarships, they'd been done trying to direct my choices. I could hear that edge of disapproval in their voices, still, all these years later. I could have done better, supposedly.

My grandmother cared, but it had been a good while since I'd talked to her. I had no girlfriend. Hell, I hadn't had a romantic interest for several years. Was that what it was? Catalina's concern felt like caring, and I didn't want to attribute more to it than was actually there. I had helped her out of a situation and gotten hurt for it. It didn't mean she cared for me specifically. She would care for anyone that had rescued her, right?

She turned her head up to me, her dark eyes catching mine, and my breath stalled in my lungs. There was just enough light from the bathroom that I could see her pupils widen. I wanted to kiss her bare lips, and that would be a very dangerous move. Firming my jaw, I drew in a deep breath.

That made it worse. This was her bed, and her room, and she was sitting directly beside me, the scent of something spicy and seductive rolling over me. And my body reacted. I'd stripped down to my athletic shorts before climbing into bed, and they weren't a lot of support. Desperately, I reached for the edge of the blanket, dragging it across my hips. What had she asked? "No, I don't think it needs ice." My gaze caught on her cheekbone, and the blossoming bruise. At least her eye hadn't completely swollen shut. "How are you doing? Did you ice that?"

One hand lifted to her cheek, and she nodded. "I did. It'll be all right."

Her expression, though. Something more was wrong. "Have you ever been hit before?"

Her eyes filled with tears and she shook her head. "I have brothers, and we played around when we were kids, but I've never dealt with something like that before. I didn't know what to do, and I was so infuriated." She swiped at her tears, then held her hand up in exasperation. "I hate that I cry when I get mad."

"It's natural," I told her softly, scrambling for a way to make it better. "You're okay."

Catalina blinked at me, and her expression crumpled a little and she nodded. Without even second-guessing myself, I tugged her into my arms and let her cry. She could call it anger or whatever, but I would hold her as she got a grip on it.

The offer of comfort backfired, though, when I realized I was taking as much comfort from the embrace as she seemed to be. Her hands wrapped around my back and her head nestled beneath my chin, some of her hair tickling my neck, but I didn't mind it. Catalina was a delicious armful, and while I hated that she'd been attacked, I didn't hate that she was taking comfort from me. I didn't hate that it had brought us together, something Virginia had been trying to do for months. The old woman had been telling me for a long time that Catalina was the woman for me, but I was nothing more than a damaged beast. She deserved so much more than what I was.

I would enjoy this moment in time for what it was; two people finding comfort in one another. If my body stayed under control, we'd be all right.

She began stroking my back, and I'm sure it was an unconscious movement, but it heated my blood. I'd been so aware of Catalina for so long, and now that I was in proximity to her, it was only getting worse. I didn't even feel the pain in my hand as I cupped her head and pressed a kiss to the top of it.

This was so dangerous. I was on the verge of pushing her away when she sagged into me even more, her unbound breasts tight against my chest. We were twisted a little awkwardly, but I don't think either of us noticed or cared.

Catalina breathed against me, and my skin...reacted. Goose-bumps raced across my shoulders and down my arms, and I wondered if she felt them. It was such an odd reaction. Then she shuddered, and lifted her head.

I'd been a Ranger for years, shaped by training and trial, and I believed I was strong, but looking down into her brilliant light brown eyes I didn't think I could maintain the distance between us. And now wasn't the time to make a move on her. She was recovering from being attacked and I was sure I was reading more into the situation than was there.

Lifting her head, she kissed me, and my world imploded.

I HAD no plans to kiss Booker, but he was looking down at me and I'd been thinking about it so long...We were already in the right position, so I just lifted my lips and covered his.

Shock roared through me at the tiny little spark of power as our lips met. Was that static? Spontaneous combustion? One soul connecting with another? I had no idea, but it was delicious and amazing, and more impactful than any other kiss I'd ever been part of before.

Booker knew how to kiss, though there was a hesitancy, a gentleness, to him I didn't expect. He seemed content to taste my lips and inhale my breath, his hands holding me to him. Then I realized he was using his injured hand, and I drew back. "Don't hurt yourself."

"I'm not," he said, nuzzling my cheek. Then he drew back. "Maybe it's smart that we slow down, though. This is not an ideal situation."

I cringed and turned away. "I'm sorry I made you uncomfortable."

Booker gave a short chuckle, the first time I'd heard the sound from him. "It's a good kind of discomfort."

As subtly as I could, I glanced down at his lap, but it was too dark to see anything. Still, a thrill went through me at the thought that I had aroused him. It was mutual, of course, but I didn't think he would acknowledge it.

What a swing of emotions this day had been.

Sighing, Booker shifted back, giving us each some space. I could still feel the radiating heat of his body, though. Was I seriously that hard up that I'd pounced on a wounded, vulnerable man?

I stood, smoothing my T-shirt down over my flannel sleep pants. "I'll let you get back to sleep. I'm sorry I... bothered you."

"You didn't bother me," Booker said, reaching for the prosthetic beside the night stand. I watched as he fitted the stump of his leg into the cup. Then he pushed to his feet as well. He towered over me in the dark room, but I didn't feel intimidated. Quite the opposite, actually. I wanted to walk into his arms and bury my face against his chest. Forcing myself to turn away, I headed toward the door, but he caught my arm from behind. "Catalina, I'm trying to be honorable. I don't want to take advantage of you or the situation."

"What if I want you to take advantage of me and the situation?"

The words were true and just slipped out, and his eyes widened in the dim room. Then, before I could retract them or turn away, he cupped my face in his hands and looked at me for a long moment. I'm sure I probably looked ghastly with my crazy hair and my purple face, but he leaned down to kiss me anyway. This time, though, was very different. There was no hesitation or delay, he just fucking swept me up and dominated me. If I'd had the chance I would have gasped, but his mouth was sealed too tightly to mine, his hand strong at the back of my head.

One of his hands cupped my side, and I had a flash of worry for his injured one, but he obviously didn't. Reaching around me, he brought us close, and I desperately wished I was at least four inches taller. Then I realized it didn't matter. We should have been awkwardly misaligned, but somehow my curves fit exactly to his angles. One of his hands swept down to cup my ass, and he pulled me up and into his hips.

I could feel my body soften in readiness for him, and I knew the direction I wanted this night to go. We were both beat up and hurting, but right this moment I didn't care about anything other than the feel of him against me. I'd seen him and fantasized about him enough that I didn't care what happened after this night. I just wanted this night.

"Are you sure about this, Cat? We're not too far to stop."

"Yes, we are. I've had disappointment after disappointment, Booker. Show me not all men are assholes."

He seemed to take my words as a challenge, because the next thing I knew the room was spinning and he was laying me down on the mattress. His firm mouth moved back and forth across my lips, and it hit me that I was never going to be the same after this.

Booker rested his body alongside my own, braced on one elbow. He didn't seem to be in pain any longer; he was too focused on me. "You have the most incredible breasts, full and pert," he whispered into my ear as his hand cupped one, thumb flicking over the nipple. I gasped, shifting beneath his touch, and reached up to catch his face in my hands. "If you're in pain we can stop," I panted, though it about killed me to make the offer.

Booker snorted. "There's only one part of me in pain, right

now, and it's not going to be an issue in a minute. Don't worry about me."

But I did worry about him. I had been for a long time. The solitary man didn't bother anyone, didn't ask anything from anyone, and didn't seem to have anyone to worry about him. I just saw him working on things occasionally, carrying lumber and tools. One day he'd been finagling a fridge into the next-door apartment, and his shoulders had been absolutely straining. I'd paused to watch because I'd been giving them time to get into the apartment, but really, I'd just been appreciating the few minutes of freedom to look at him.

"You have the softest skin," he murmured, running his fingers delicately down my side. Lifting my arms invitingly above my head, Booker stripped my T-shirt away. "Oh, fuck," he breathed, and I grinned with satisfaction. I loved I could provoke a reaction in the stoic man. I cupped my breasts for him, and he leaned down to kiss the soft skin of my cleavage. Then he moved to my left breast and danced his tongue over the tip.

Pleasure struck like lightning and I arched back, giving him better access. Fuck, that felt good. His free hand was playing at the elastic of my sleep pants, dipping low on the sensitive skin, then up and along the edge of the fabric. He was teasing me, building me up, but I was ready for him. My body had gone fluid, tingling with expectation.

Shimmying, I worked my pants down my hips, along with my panties. He helped me get them off my feet and tossed them away.

Then he shifted over me, his hips aligning with mine, and pure arousal flowed through me. The feel of his erection made me gasp, and I lifted my knees up around his hips.

Booker rocked against my pelvic bone, and I knew it was

going to be a ride I wouldn't soon forget. He went still for a moment, and a subtle shiver rippled over him.

"There are condoms in the bedside table," I whispered. If we didn't do it now, I had a feeling it would get skipped. I was covered for pregnancy because I had an IUD, but we hadn't had a chance to talk about anything more immediate.

Booker rolled away and dug in the bedside table, finding a strip of condoms. Then he turned, and I got a full view of his body. He was absolutely the biggest, most strongly built man I'd ever been with, and that erection... It was hard and beautiful, stretching long and straight, and I worried, because he was definitely the biggest man I'd ever been with. The condom rolled on, but it looked tight.

Booker glanced at me, then, remarkably, he flushed, like he was embarrassed. "If you've changed your mind, we can stop." His voice was even deeper than normal, like he'd been screaming at a concert for hours, but I understood his words.

I shook my head. "No, I haven't changed my mind."

Then, to my mortification, I blushed as well. And I knew by the grin that spread on his face that he saw it. Shit...

Well, it was our first time together, so awkwardness was to be expected. I laughed, covering my breasts with my hands and praying nothing else jiggled too much. When I looked up, Booker was grinning as well, and seemed a little bemused at the situation.

"I hope you're not laughing at me," he murmured.

I shook my head, drawing in a deep breath. "No, just the situation."

With a final adjustment to the condom, he moved toward the bed, and I opened my arms, excitement surging in a fresh wave. The man was absolutely gorgeous, and I knew I would enjoy this ride.

"Catalina..." he hesitated.

Grinning, I cocked my head at him. "You keep trying to get away, and I can't tell if it's for my benefit or because you don't want to be here. Or maybe you're in pain and just don't want to admit it."

He settled back into the cradle of my hips. "I definitely want to be here. Yes, there's pain, but it's inconsequential. I guess I'm just a little shocked you want to be with me. I'm not the type of guy I thought you'd go for."

I looked up at him, incredulous. "Are you serious? Why would I not want to be with you? You're gorgeous and you seem to be an actual nice person."

He shook his head and didn't answer, and I didn't press him. There was too much talking going on, anyway. I shifted my legs around his hips and looked down his length. He was thrilled to be where he was.

"I need you, Booker," I told him softly, reaching down. Booker jerked at the touch of my fingers around his length. With a hiss, he pressed forward, and I guided him in.

Oh, hell... I thought I was ready for him, but the deeper he pushed... I moaned as he filled me, then filled me even fuller. He paused, but I didn't think he was completely seated yet. "Give me just a sec," I whispered.

Booker braced his elbows beside my head and began to brush kisses down over my cheeks, avoiding my bruise. At the same time he started doing this gentle wave thing with his hips, pulling back then pressing forward again, getting my body used to his.

I shifted my hips up to meet him each time, and pleasure began to build, easing the way for him.

"You feel...like a dream," he whispered, levering up to brace on his arms.

I looked at the muscle bunched around me, from his straining biceps, the mounds of his pecs and down the cobbles of his stomach. Booker had more strength than any five men I knew, but he touched me like I was made of spun sugar.

"Hey," I whispered in his right ear, nipping gently. He shuddered, and I could tell he was listening. "I want you to fuck me."

There was an infinitesimal hesitation, then he pressed all the way forward. This time, I could tell he didn't hold back. I felt more full than I ever had before, and it was delicious. Then he drew back and began to move, and my body responded. It usually took me a good while to get warmed up, but not with Booker. Within just a couple of minutes, my body was dancing on the edge of orgasm.

Then he reached down and lifted my thighs even higher, toward my shoulders, and the orgasm that had been slowly building slammed into me. I might have screamed a little. I know I dug my fingernails into his ass cheeks, but I couldn't help it.

The pleasure consumed every part of me, rippling through my body over and over again. Then I felt him lose rhythm, and I knew he was close as well. Tightening my body as much as I was able, I looked up into his eyes. "I want you to come for me."

Booker's face contorted, harsh with pleasure, as his orgasm took over his movements. I wrapped my arms around his shoulders as he came, pressing kisses where I could reach. And when he went lax in my arms, I held him for as long as I could before he headed to the bathroom to dispose of the condom. When he returned to the bed, he lifted his arm and I curled against him, determined to get the most out of the night, because I had a feeling the light of day would change everything.

6

I knew before I opened my eyes that Booker was gone.

There was a chill to the bed. An emptiness. All night I'd slept cuddled next to him, breathing in his scent, and it hadn't been enough. I wanted to cry that he was gone, but I refused. He'd stayed the night because I'd insisted, and now he and his dog had moved on.

Had I been too clingy? That was a distinct possibility. It was too late to change my behavior now. I'd acted the way I'd wanted to, needed to, and I'd had a wondrous night, in spite of what we were healing. Though he hadn't said anything, I hope he had as well.

I looked for a note, but there was nothing. Though, if he wasn't familiar with my apartment, especially in the dark, I doubted he would have been able to find a Post-it pad or anything.

He could have woken me though.

At ten a.m., a plumber arrived to fix my clogged toilet. Bill was his name, and he grinned at everything. He explained that Booker had sent him to unclog a toilet and showed me the texts from Booker that morning. I let him through to the bathroom, then went back to look at the broken door. I wondered if I need to call a construction firm, or a handyman, or something, to fix it.

Not what I wanted to deal with today.

Within just a few minutes Bill came out to the kitchen, where I was brewing a cup of coffee.

"Ma'am, I know what caused the blockage."

I looked at the older man. He wore bright red suspenders, though he wasn't very big. Trying to fight the plumber ass-crack stereotype, maybe? He was grinning as he held up a clear plastic Ziplock bag.

"Is that a..."

"Yup. Looks like the wheel off a toy tractor."

Chris had had a tractor he was playing with. Had he broken it, then tried to hide the evidence? It sounded like something he would do. The wheel was about the size of a donut, but flexible, and about an inch wide.

"Thank you so much for that," I said, taking the bag. I doubted there was any way to fix the tractor, but if I showed him the wheel maybe I could have a talk with him about what to dispose of where.

The sweet plumber disappeared down the hallway. I was just about to close the door when another man appeared, a tool-belt slung low over his narrow hips. He appeared to be much younger, with dark hair and dancing hazel eyes. I had never seen him before, because I would have definitely remembered him. Damn.

"Ms. Rivera? My name is Tanner. Building management sent me up to fix your door, at least short-term. Do you mind if I come in?"

I looked into his eyes and only saw honesty. But, I had checked with the plumber too. "Tanner? Who hired you?"

"Yes, ma'am, Tanner. Management, ma'am," the young man

grinned again. "Booker called me early this morning and told me you were a priority and to drop everything to do this." He surveyed the door. "And I can see why. Damn..."

Dropping down onto his knees, he surveyed the damage, pulling away pieces of shattered wood. Then he looked up at me, and I knew what he was going to say. "It all has to be replaced, huh?"

"Yes, ma'am. And I know I'm going to have to go to the building supply store because I don't have what I need on my truck. It'll take me most of today to get it done."

I sighed, nodding. "That's fine. Do I need to be here?"

He shook his head. "No, ma'am. I'll secure the door as much as I can if you have something to do."

I needed to go to the prosecutor's office to file for a restraining order, not something I was looking forward to. I really didn't want Sean out and about before I got my door fixed. "Is there any way I can reinforce this door? An ex kicked it in, last night, and I don't want it to happen again."

Tanner gave me an understanding look. "Booker already talked to me about that. Yes, I'm going to put in a heavier steel door that won't be able to be kicked in. It'll take me the day to build the casement, though, then fit the door."

"Okay. Do what you need to do. What's this going to cost me?"

Tanner shook his head. "Booker told me the bill goes to him."

Hm. We'd have to talk about that.

While Tanner measured and did his handyman stuff, I got ready to go to town, anxiety churning in my gut.

I really didn't want to adult today...

∾

I FOUGHT my anxiety as I watched Catalina pull away. Blue leaned against my leg, sensing that I needed something and doing what he could to help. He watched her drive away as well, ears pricked.

It seemed presumptuous that she would need or want me to be there at the courthouse, but I worried. Her ex was probably still in jail, but there was always the slightest chance that he'd gotten out and would be on the lookout for her. Maybe I should go down anyway because I'd been a part of apprehending the asshole in the middle of the assault.

Fuck. I hated this indecision.

If anything happened to her...

"Blue, stay," I told him, snatching up my keys. I shut the door behind me and headed for my truck.

I spent an hour in my truck outside the Franklin County Prosecuting attorney's office, watching for either Catalina or Sean to appear. Eventually, Cat appeared, looking haggard and withdrawn, her curly dark hair drawn back into a low ponytail. She wore black pants, a pale-colored shirt and a dark blazer. Calm, sedate clothes for the courtroom. She hadn't done anything to hide the purple bruise across her face, though, and I was proud of her for that. They needed to see what he'd done to her.

Her head was up, though, and her chin high as she walked down the sidewalk on the other side of the street. She looked strong and beautiful to me. Scenes from the previous night flitted through my brain.

If it wasn't for the throbbing in my hand and stomach, I would have thought that last night had been a dream. I could feel the difference in my body, though, and I knew what had happened. I had made love to a beautiful woman, a woman I'd been fantasizing about for a long time.

My body was clamoring for more. It had been through a dry

spell and it seemed to sense that more relief was near, because I'd been hard all morning. I'd been hard for Catalina, though. The woman had been creative and eager and caring, and I was still fighting guilt over giving in. It hadn't been the right time or the right setting. She had definitely been the right woman, though. And other than the initial surprise, she hadn't really paid any attention to my amputation. I was still a little shocked by that.

Damn.

Catalina Rivera had rocked my world, and I was struggling with keeping my distance. It was the right thing to do, but it wasn't what I *wanted* to do.

I watched as she crossed the street and got into her car. Then I watched as she rested her head on the steering wheel. Was she crying? Fuck. Every fiber of my being screamed at me I needed to go comfort her, but I made myself stay in the truck. She was physically safe. That was what was important.

This morning I'd woken in fear, my heart in my throat as I replayed getting blown up in Afghanistan. It was the incident that had sent me home with one leg, and I would remember it for the rest of my life. It made sense that I would dream about it, considering the concussion and the kick to the leg, but I'd woken up aggressive, wanting to beat the hell out of something again. Kicking Sean's ass had felt good yesterday, no lie. And if I saw him on the street, I wasn't sure I wouldn't kick it again. It had been a long time since I'd been physically aggressive, and it had actually felt good to let go.

Catalina viewed me as a hero, though, and that was so fucked. I was not a hero.

The radio had been playing in the background, and something about a veteran caught my attention. I turned the dial up.

Ah. It was just a teaser for the Love Vixen show, which

would air in a few hours. Should have known. But it was promoting a veteran asking for help. Hm...

I squarely blamed Virginia for me even knowing about the damn show, and I knew she was trying to get me to loosen up or get in touch with my emotions, or something. Every time I went up to her apartment to fix whatever little thing she'd noticed, the show was playing. Or reruns of the show. I'd gone up one day to replace a lightbulb and her apartment was full of people, and they were all listening with rapt attention to some woman pleading for help from the fictitious Vixen. I doubted there was any such woman. It was probably a group of middle-aged white men telling women what they thought they needed to hear so they could sell sex-toy advertisements during the breaks.

Catalina lifted her head and wiped her face, and it broke my heart that she'd been crying.

Starting her Toyota SUV, she merged into traffic and took off. I didn't feel like I needed to watch over her, so I turned in the opposite direction and headed for home. I stopped at Blue's favorite pet store on my way and bought a bag of food, some treats, and a couple of toys. They would be shredded in hours, but he appreciated anything new.

I didn't see Catalina's car in the lot when I pulled in, but I wasn't worried. She'd probably needed to stop for something as well. I unpacked the dog supplies and gave Blue a new Kong, stuffed with rotisserie chicken.

Then I sank down into my recliner and tipped my head back, closing my eyes. The manager's apartment was on the bottom floor and I could hear everyone enter through the front door. Catalina, whether she realized it or not, had a very distinctive jingle to her keychain and the cadence of her steps. And sometimes she was muttering to herself. Blue always went to the door to listen to her.

I closed my eyes and tried to pretend I wasn't waiting for her.

~

As I juggled my heavy grocery bag, I opened the door of my little mailbox. Just a bill and two offers for credit cards. No, thank you. Moving down the hallway, I punched the button for the elevator. It was going on five o'clock, so I was really hoping my door had been replaced.

The elevator had just arrived when something big and black jostled me from the side. "What the… oh, hey, Blue."

The big dog was wiggling his butt, along with his short, tiny stub of tail. For some reason, he seemed especially happy to see me. I glanced around for Booker.

"Blue!"

"He's down here," I called, blocking the doors of the elevator. I looked back at the dog. "You wouldn't even give me the time of day, yesterday. Why do you like me now? Because I smell like your owner?"

My heart raced at the prospect of seeing Booker. I'd thought about our night together and knew that it wasn't a mistake. But I worried he thought it was. Yes, it had been spur of the moment, but that didn't make it wrong. And I didn't want him to think I'd slept with him because he saved me, or out of pity or anything. I slept with him because it was him.

There he was, swinging around the corner of the hallway, boots and jeans and T-shirt fitting him like they were painted on. And he didn't move with any irregularity. I couldn't even tell he wore a prosthetic. The bandage was still on his hand, at least. The light caught the shine of his light brown hair, and I had a flashback of running my fingers through it at some point. The curls were soft and thick.

This ground floor area was mostly maintenance and management. There was a laundry area down here, as well as some storage for the residents, our mailboxes. And Booker's office and apartment were down here, as well as a couple of resident spaces on the other side. Oh, and the door to the outside courtyard was off to the left, where they just came from. Blue must have been going potty.

I stroked the dog's head with my free hand and he leaned into my leg. That was nice. Not sure what had changed, but I was happy with it. Maybe the dog was schizophrenic and the scary, stalking beast would be out later.

Booker met my gaze as he stopped in front of me. "Hey."

"Hey. How are you feeling?"

"Fine," he bit out, reaching for my heavy reusable bag. "I was just heading up to your place to see if Tanner's done. He texted me a few minutes ago."

"Good," I said, stepping back so that he could get on the elevator. I let him take the bag, because it was hurting my hand. "I was tired of killing time."

"What the hell is in this thing?" he asked, glancing down into the opening.

"Liquor for the Love Vixen party. It's at Virginia's tonight."

Every Friday someone in the building, usually Virginia, hosted a party to listen to the weekly Love Vixen podcast. I had promised her I would get the booze and pop she'd requested.

Booker didn't roll his eyes, but it was a near thing. I almost laughed out loud. "Don't knock it till you try it. The Love Vixen has pretty solid advice."

"I know, that's what Virginia tells me too." He paused and glanced at her. "So, you weren't home?" he asked, moving to the opposite corner from me.

Why was he acting so strange? "No. I went in and filed the protection order paperwork against Sean, then went to a coffee shop to work. I didn't expect to get anything done here today, and I needed wi-fi."

"You're a website designer?"

I glanced at him. This conversation was so weird. I was a little surprised he didn't ask me about the protection order. The elevator had taken off, but it didn't feel like it was moving at all. "Yes. I design websites and do logo work. Graphic design."

"That's cool."

He folded his hands in front of himself, still holding the liquor bag, and looked up at the numbers. We arrived on my floor and he held an arm out to keep the elevator door open. I walked down the hall toward my door, Blue at my side. The dog had latched on to me for some reason.

Tanner was standing at my open door, grinning. "You're back in business, ma'am. Nothing is getting through this door unless you open it yourself."

I moved close so I could test the door. It latched perfectly, and I couldn't tell that the casement wasn't wood. It fit into the rest of the building seamlessly.

"The paint might be a little tacky, but it should dry within a few hours."

As soon as he said that, I wanted to touch the paint just to check. I snorted, curling my fingers into my hand. "It looks incredible. Thank you so much for working on it. I know you had other work to do today."

"Nothing more important than this," Booker said, surprising me. His expression was slightly fierce, brows furrowed and his arms crossed over his chest. I would think that would hurt his belly wound, but maybe not...

"Yeah, what he said," Tanner grinned, his blue eyes flashing. "This is a Fortress door, so nothing will get through it. You've got double dead-bolt locks as well as a door barricade on the inside." He unlocked the door and led me inside, crouching to show me a small piece of metal at the bottom of the door. "This is a barricade. At night you flip this down and no one is coming in."

I flicked it down with my toe, then back up. It was perfect.

"Thank you so much, Tanner. I really do appreciate it."

"No problem, ma'am," he said, dropping a small ring of keys into my palm. "If you have any problems, just let Booker or I know. I left my card on your counter."

"Thank you. I will," I promised.

The young guy grabbed up a few tools, stowed them in his canvas bag and was gone. Booker grabbed the handles of the booze bag and carried it in. "Lock it from the inside," he told me, and I did. Then I dropped the barricade piece. Yeah, this fucker wasn't moving.

I turned to him, grinning. "I feel so much better, now. Thank you for having Tanner work on it."

I stepped forward and went up on tiptoes to wrap my arms around his neck in a hug. Booker bent down for me and wrapped an arm around my back for support, but when I would have drawn back, he held me close. Leaning back a little, I looked up into his eyes. "We should really talk about last night."

"I know," he said. Then he kissed me.

Damn it. Everything I'd wanted to say went out of my head when his mouth touched mine, and I lost myself in the kiss. This is what I'd been waiting for since this morning when I woke up alone. Maybe he had too? At least a little?

Booker straightened, lifting me easily off the ground as he continued to kiss me, his tongue gliding against mine. It seemed natural to lift my legs up around his hips. Immediately, his hands cupped my ass and he walked us to the couch. One moment we were vertical, the next I was gasping in a breath as we landed on the cushions.

"Sorry," he said, then ground himself into my pelvis.

"Ohmygosh..." I breathed, shifting on the cushions. They kind of wrapped around me and made it hard to move like I wanted to. "Booker," I sighed.

My fingers buried in his hair as he shifted down, his hands roving over my body. Again, I worried about his injury, but he obviously didn't feel it. I felt my shirt get lifted and pushed above my breasts under my chin, and I laughed. "Hold on before you strangle me."

Bracing himself on his hands and knees above me, he waited as I stripped off my shirt and bra. I would let him do the rest.

His bright green eyes had gone dark with arousal as he looked down at me, and I had to take it in. Yeah, men always wanted sex and the package didn't always matter as long as they could get off, but I could tell by looking at Booker's expression that he genuinely liked my shape. Sean had always made little digs about my size and commented on everything I ate, which was why he never even made it close to my bed. Yes. I was a voluptuous girl and yes, I liked food. The important thing was, I was healthy and strong. I jogged regularly and worked out at the gym three times a week.

Booker didn't have an inch of fat on him. I ran my hands down his sides and beneath his shirt, avoiding the bandage on his stomach. "That has to hurt, with you braced like that."

One side of his mouth tipped up in a grin. "I feel no pain right now, I promise you."

That grin... no matter what happened, that grin was worth everything. I couldn't remember ever seeing him smile, with teeth, and especially not at me. It seemed like he was always glowering at me, or frowning. I would love to see him laugh.

Rocking back on his knees, Booker looked down my length, then he reached out and cupped my hips. Normally I would have felt self-conscious having a man look at me like that, but I had seen the appreciation in his eyes, and it didn't feel fake. His fingers went to the waistband of my jeans and he unfastened them, then began tugging on the fabric. I lifted my hips enough that he could pull them off. I thought he would take the panties, too, but he didn't. Instead, he tossed the jeans away, sat back on his knees, and ran his hands down my hips again.

"You have the most amazing skin. And I can't get enough of your hips."

Freaking tears came to my eyes, because it was a struggle to be my size and not feel self-conscious most of the time. I worked out and did what I could to eat healthy, but there was a certain amount of genetics working against me. If I was just a few inches taller... No, I was me and I'd quit hoping for more height long ago.

Seeing that look in his eyes, though... that was something I would remember for a long time.

Booker squeezed my hips one more time, then ran his fingers down the cleft of my hip. My panties were already soaked because my body knew what pleasure was coming. One of his fingers stroked beneath the elastic, brushing against me, and I huffed out a breath. *Please go deeper...please go deeper...*

Then one finger slipped through the swollen folds of my body, and I gasped at the sensation. Booker was the strong, silent type, but he definitely knew what to do with a woman's body. Tugging the panties aside, he delved deeper, finding the perfect place to stroke while his thumb circled my clit. It felt sublime, and within seconds I was crying out with release, my thighs tightening around his hand.

Booker bent over and teased my right nipple with his tongue, spurring a fresh wave of release. My eyes were shut and my head buried in the cushion, so his touch was the focal point of my world, and he completely rocked my foundations.

When I could catch my breath, I opened my eyes and found him grinning above me, his mouth spread wide, teeth gleaming. "I think you might have passed out for a second."

I laughed in response, thrilled to see the look on his face. "I think you might be right. I'm back now, though, and I'm still aching."

Booker reached down with one hand and unfastened his jeans, shoving them down his hips.

"That's good enough," I told him, pulling him down on top of me.

Booker didn't argue, and when he settled into the cradle of my hips, his dick seemed to know exactly where to go. He slid deep, and we groaned together at the feel of being locked as one. Then he began to move, and the pleasure spiked. He rode me hard, and within just a couple of minutes we were both orgasming. I'd never orgasmed at the same time as my partner before, so that was really something.

Then he melted my heart as he rolled to his side against the couch back and took me with him, arms shifting my limp body perfectly. He cradled my head on his bicep.

"Thank you," I told him softly.

His chest jerked with a laugh. "I think I should be thanking you," he murmured, voice incredibly deep.

"That's not what I mean," I sighed. "The sex was exceptional, of course, but I appreciate you getting the contractors out here and everything, too. It wasn't something I wanted to deal with today."

He stroked my back with his hand, and I sagged into him.

"So, tell me about this morning. Did you get your protection order?"

"Yes," I said, moving my head back so I could look up at him. "I literally had to go in front of the judge, though, in a courtroom, and explain why I was in fear of my life."

Booker reached out and pressed a kiss to my forehead. "That had to have been hard."

My heart warmed with the sign of affection. "I wish you'd have been there," I admitted.

"I was, kind of."

"What?" I drew back to look at him again.

He shifted and frowned. "I didn't...I just watched over you outside. Made sure no one was there to bother you."

Fuck, he was going to kill me. My eyes filled with tears and I leaned into him, my throat tight. "You were downtown with me?"

"Yes. I made sure you drove away fine and I expected you to come home. I didn't know you'd gone to the coffee shop or whatever."

I heard what he didn't want to admit. "I'm sorry I made you worry."

His arms tightened around me and he pulled me tight against him. We stayed like that for a good while, just being close to one another, listening to the other breathe. I was the one that finally shifted.

"Virginia is going to come looking for me if I don't get down there to help her."

I untangled myself and rolled off the couch, giggling because I had an incredible wedgie and Blue chose that moment to come say hi. I pushed him away, giggling. "Get Booker, not me," I gasped.

Booker was sprawled on the couch, boots on, jeans half off, looking freshly fucked. His dick should not have been impressive at that point, but it totally still was. And I had a feeling if I stuck around any longer we'd be going at it again.

I needed to get ready, damn it. With a regretful look over my shoulder, I headed down the hallway toward my bedroom.

7

I could fuck her again, right this second, I decided as I watched her walk down the hallway, her ass cheeks jiggling. The woman had a shape built for fucking, curvy and voluptuous. And there was a glint of moisture at the back of her thighs.

For the first time in my life, I'd been so aroused by a woman that I'd forgotten to put a damn condom on. I had a fresh one in my wallet. Catalina had them by the bed. But my brain had completely spaced out on that step, too focused on the pleasure to be had between her thighs.

What the fuck was I doing here? I had nothing to offer her. Catalina was the kind of woman that would want kids and commitment. She would be a fantastic mother. Those genes didn't run in my family. My dad had been a manic mess, too absorbed in his own perceived glory, and my mother had never challenged him. I don't remember him ever actually asking me if I liked football. And to be fair, I did love the sport, for a long time. He'd just driven me too hard. It was easy to see, looking back.

I grinned. Catalina would challenge anyone, and kick their

ass. She was a hell of a woman. But she had sense to go with it.

An ache settled in my chest. Ignoring it, I stood from the couch and got dressed. Then I wasn't sure what to do. Should I wait for her here? Was it presumptuous to go back to the bedroom to tell her I was leaving?

Blue took the decision out of my hands, jogging back the hallway toward the bedroom. I followed the dog, grinning when I found Catalina on the bed, fighting off a six-inch Doberman tongue. She was giggling like crazy, temptingly half-dressed as she tried to push him away. The dog probably weighed damn near what she did, though, and he was persistent. Blue's perception of Cat had changed since yesterday, and I worried that the dog was going to become attached as well.

"Blue," I said, trying to be stern. The dog looked at me but didn't seem especially concerned. There hadn't been a lot of command in my voice.

Catalina took the pause in the attack and pushed to her feet, laughing. She'd been trying to get a pair of socks on, apparently. Once she got them on, she went back for the shirt that was waiting for her. I watched her breasts as she lifted her arms and dropped the fabric over. I couldn't help but be a little disappointed when they were hidden.

"We should probably let you get to Virginia's."

Catalina moved to the bathroom doorway and disappeared, then reappeared brushing her hair. It looked a little damp, like she'd put something in it to tame down the curls. She drew it back into a ponytail, twirled it around somehow and had a pretty knot at the base of her neck. Then she pulled a few tendrils of hair out to curl around her face.

Damn. From a distance she was beautiful. Close up she was even more so, her skin milky smooth. I need to get out of here.

"If you need anything, I want you to call me immediately."

"I will," she promised. Then she walked across the room to

stand in front of me. "I've enjoyed our time together, Booker. And I want to see you again, without all the craziness going on."

My heart leaped in my chest and I wanted to reach out to her, but I kept my hands at my sides. She deserved so much better than a beat up guy like me, with all my issues.

"We'll see, Catalina," I said, and I knew my voice was too gruff. I stroked a piece of her hair behind her ear. "I think you can do better than a beat-up old Ranger. Go listen to your Love Vixen, or whatever she's called."

Cat smiled, but her eyes were shadowed. She seemed to sense that I was withdrawing. But her lips tipped up in a smile. "Okay. If you need anything, please let me know."

"Blue," I said as I turned away.

I got to the door and the dog wasn't at heel. When I looked back the hallway, I could see him peering at me like I was forgetting something. "Heel," I said again. With a backward glance into the bedroom, Blue came to heel and we left the apartment. I pulled the steel door closed behind me, and tried not to wince.

This was for the best.

I REFUSED TO CRY. Instead, I went into the bathroom and applied my makeup, just like I would any other time I was going to Virginia's. She would see through the armor, though, and I wasn't sure I wanted to talk about it at the party.

Shit... the Vixen was probably going to make me cry, too.

Maybe I had misread that goodbye. I really hoped I had.

I grabbed the bag of alcohol and soda pop. Then I got my big aluminum cup and filled it with ice water. Liquor would make me even more emotional, and I didn't need that tonight.

When I stepped off the elevator, I could see that Virginia's door was propped open.

"Hello," I called, pushing through.

"Come on in!"

Virginia stood at the kitchen sink washing some dishes. She set a cup in the drainer and turned to face me. At about 5'6", even she was taller than me, but she was only about half my size, and there was a gentleness to her that some elderly women grew into. She wasn't helpless, but she was the kind of woman who would rather let a man do something for her than get her hands dirty.

With perfectly coiffed, bright white hair, and glasses perched on her nose, she seemed like the perfect grandma. But she was alone in the world. Her husband had passed years ago, and her sons as well. She had one niece who lived down south and only visited occasionally. Virginia considered the Willows her roost, and she needed to take care of the chicks. Hence, the weekly get-togethers to listen to the Love Vixen and socialize. Sometimes she dragged out old-school board games. We'd spent hours one night fighting over Monopoly. And I had to admit, since Evie had gone to Guyana it was nice to have the social interaction.

People weren't obligated to attend, but for the most part, it was a fun time. Around the holidays she made sure everyone had a place to go, and we, in turn, did the same for her.

Virginia turned and reached out to give me a hug, the smile huge on her face. "Hello, my sweet Cat. Oh, dear, look at that bruise. I hope they keep that man in jail a long time."

"Me too," I admitted, though it was hard to know with the Ohio justice system. It seemed like they were always over-crowded and releasing criminals early.

"And is Booker okay? I tried to hold people off, but Mr. Lumpkin has that leak in his roof, now."

"Booker is fine. I'm sure he'll get to it soon, if he didn't already."

Virginia's eyes narrowed and she cocked her head, staring at me hard. "What?"

I shook my head, my throat tightening down with emotion. Damn old woman saw too much. "Nothing."

She made a circle with her finger, pointing at my face. "That is not nothing. This is...love drama."

I sighed, knowing that she wouldn't let up until I told her something. "Yes, but I don't want to talk about it tonight. I'll come over tomorrow or something."

She cupped my face in her damp hands. "I won't bug you about it, then."

Leaning in, I gave her another hug, holding her tight for a long minute. The woman had been through more strife than I could imagine in her life, but she still looked for the romance and love in the world. It was why the Vixen parties were so important to her. And it was why we, the residents, all took turns attending.

"Thank you for being you, Virginia."

She grinned at me as I pulled back. "No problem, darling. Did you bring my soda?"

"I did."

It was a nice group that attended the party that night. Ms. Gamble, the teacher from the top floor, Angelique from 6A looking casually chic in her skinny black workout pants and sweatshirt, Mr. Nguyen from 3D and his granddaughter Jen. Mr. and Mrs. Utz came, as well as Ms. Hatch, the newest resident. Then there was a final knock on the door and Tanner walked in, carrying a store-bought container of cookies and looking a little out of place.

I gave him a little wave and a smile, and he wandered over after he set the cookie container on the counter.

"Everyone, this is Tanner. He does door work for Booker."

There was a round of hellos, which sent a wash of color over his cheeks. He walked across the room and sat on one of the dining room chairs that had been turned to face the living room. "So, what do we do? I don't even really know why I'm here. I just saw this woman downstairs and she told me to come tonight."

I laughed. "Virginia is a sweet lady and she's always trying to encourage love. She probably also told you that there would be several single ladies here. And free food."

Tanner grinned. "She did. But I came because she said you would be here and that you were single."

I swallowed, at a loss as to what to say. "Thanks, Tanner. I'm single, but... it's complicated."

Tanner gave me a surprisingly understanding smile. "Yeah, I thought so. If it ever gets uncomplicated, maybe you can keep me in mind."

"I will," I grinned, knowing that I totally wouldn't. Tanner seemed like a nice guy, but he also seemed very young to me. I liked them more mature and experienced. "Angelique is single, though, and Jen is as well," I tipped my chin in their directions and Tanner gave me an appreciative look. "Ms. Gamble is as well if you like them a little older."

But he had already set his sights on the most difficult woman in the room, Angelique. "Mind if I..."

"You go, buddy. Just know she has claws."

Not looking deterred, Tanner crossed the room to get a drink, which put him in closer proximity to my tall, blonde, aloof neighbor.

"Okay, we're about ready," Virginia said, her voice excited. "Get your drinks and snacks and I'll turn Berny on."

Bernadette was a former neighbor that still called in on Messenger to take part in the Friday night ritual podcast listening party. We all waved at her when she came on screen. Then Virginia shushed us. "It's starting."

They listened to the canned music leading into the Love

Vixen podcast, her sexy, alto voice giving a short teaser about the upcoming listener-sent questions.

"*This is going to be the first podcast in a special military series we're building,*" the Vixen said, voice husky and concise. "*Every month we will take one Friday to recognize advice requests for the men and women of our armed services, and I can tell you, I've read some of these letters already, and they're going to tug at those heartstrings.*

"*First up, we have Tongue-tied in Tucson. Dear Love Vixen, there is this sexy sweet ex-military guy that comes in to work every Wednesday. He has the most haunted eyes. I know his coffee order by heart. I get tongue tied and can't get a word out. I am normally not that shy. Any suggestions on how to get his attention without looking crazy?*"

There were a few 'aws' from around the room, and I took a sip of my water. I only half paid attention to the responses until I heard the Vixen give a trigger warning.

"*Dear Love Vixen- I am a Marine. Served my country for 15 years. I am now transitioning to civilian life again and want to get back into the dating scene. The thing is, while on a mission I lost a limb. Not the one that women enjoy the most, though. So help a guy out, are you available? I would love to get to know you and show you what makes Marines the best.*"

The Love Vixen, laughing, dodged the flirt and gave him advice about getting back out into society, but it got me thinking. Had I reacted badly to Booker's amputation? I thought I'd rolled with the shock pretty well last night, considering, but maybe I hadn't. Or should I have made over it more? I wasn't sure exactly how to react to that. I knew that a lot of vets didn't appreciate the 'thank you for your service' bit because they didn't feel like they deserved it and it sometimes came across as patronizing.

This wasn't a situation I ever expected to be in. The only

experience I'd had with amputations had been a great grandfather with diabetes, and a cousin who'd lost a leg in a motorcycle crash. Frank had seen his amputation as a mark of pride, and he'd had no hesitation in pulling off his lower leg for pranks at Christmas. Booker didn't seem to be the type to be that... carefree.

I split out of there early, but not before Virginia pulled me aside. "Come talk to me when you get a chance," she said, holding my hands.

"I will," I promised.

I went up the elevator, down the hallway and through my new door, feeling restless. I didn't like feeling this way, as if something was unfinished. I thought back to a few hours ago in the bedroom. We'd just made love, and he'd turned indifferent. Cold. I didn't understand.

The last thing he'd said to me had seemed like a goodbye. Was I wrong?

Before I could change my mind, I pulled on my tennis shoes, grabbed my keys and headed downstairs. I went past the mailboxes and laundry to the door marked Building Manager and knocked. Blue woofed from the other side of the door, and I grinned. At least I knew one of them liked me.

Booker opened the door, and I about swooned. He'd just taken a shower and his hair was dark with moisture. There was a wet towel draped around his shoulders and he only wore low-slung jeans around his hips. No shirt. So his impressive six-pack was on display, stitches and all, running diagonally from the right peck to the left hipbone.

His green eyes flared with something when he saw me, then he looked away. Had that been need? Desire? It had been wistful, definitely.

"I don't think you were supposed to get those wet." Then I realized something else. "You're listening to the Love Vixen?"

Booker scowled, crossing his arms defensively. "There was something on there I wanted to hear."

I wasn't going to bust his balls about it. Maybe it would make him a more approachable man. "I didn't like the way we left things."

Booker frowned, looking down at the ground. "I'm sorry about that."

I waited for more, but he shut his mouth and didn't say anything else. "I feel like we could do more."

Finally, he looked at me. "I don't think we should get involved."

My brows jerked up. "Aren't we already involved? I don't understand."

His eyes connected with mine and I frowned. They'd gone chilly again. "Yes, we were involved for a minute. But we're not going to go any further. I think we should stay friends."

I drew back, feeling a little betrayed. And seriously hurt. Booker had had my back for two days, but suddenly I wasn't enough.

That's probably what it was. He wanted to be done with me and he was very nicely trying to step back. *Get a grip, Cat, and take control of your own life.*

"Thanks for the help this week," I told him, my voice flat. "If you need anything, you know where I am."

Turning on my heel, I headed for the elevator. Blue's whine filled my ears before I turned the corner. I prayed the elevator was still on this floor, because I didn't know how long I would be able to hold my tears. Virginia's party would probably be letting out soon, and I didn't want to run into anyone if I could avoid it.

Thankfully, I made it all the way to my place before the tears began to fall.

It took me two days to get up the courage to go see Virginia. I'd been dumped before, but this felt different. This felt...like a piece of me had been left behind. And I didn't understand why.

A few months ago I'd been banned by Facebook, my main platform for social media and marketing. No matter how many emails or messages I sent, I'd never gotten a reason for the banning. So, I didn't know what I'd done wrong in the first place. I was just left wondering.

This was the same kind of thing. All of my body-image insecurities flooded back. Unless Booker came up and told me what exactly I'd done, I would always be left wondering. Which meant I would always second-guess myself with other relationships.

It was a vicious circle.

Virginia seemed to sense that I was down, because she drew me into a hug as soon as she saw me on the other side of her door. I fought furiously to keep the tears from my eyes, but I was sure she knew.

"Come in, dear. Oh, your face is looking much better."

I touched the cheekbone. The serious bruising had faded, leaving a yellowish haze under my skin. It wasn't perfect, but it was getting better.

"Let me get the iced tea."

We sat at the dining room table. Virginia served me iced tea and set a plate of butter cookies between us. They looked good, so I ate one. Then another. Then I very deliberately pushed them away.

"Those cookies aren't going to keep you from telling me what's going on."

"I know," I breathed out. "I just don't know where to start."

Virginia took a sip of her tea. "Tell me about Sean."

So, I did. And that naturally flowed into what had happened after. Virginia had a great knack for listening, and encouraging with strategically placed silences. I ended up telling her everything.

"Times have changed since I fell in love with my Chuck," she said with a sigh. "I can't pretend to know what you're thinking, but I don't feel like Booker is a bad bet. He has depths I don't think anyone understands, even himself. I worry about how alone he is."

"I do too," I sighed. "And I thought I was kind of getting to know him, but he shut me down. He has a prosthetic leg. Did you know that?"

Virginia nodded. "I thought so. I never asked him about it, though."

"He lost it in Afghanistan, but that's all I know. Anyway, I didn't know he had a prosthetic. I didn't run screaming when I saw it or anything, but I was surprised. I'm not sure if he's shutting us down because of the way I reacted or what. It's the only thing I can think of."

Virginia smiled. "It's hard to tell why men do the things they do, but I will say, he's very protective of you. Maybe you got too close."

"Me?" I looked at her, incredulous. "Since when? I've only talked to the man in-depth just recently. He would barely give me the time of day any other time."

"He admires you making a life for yourself and not relying on anyone else. Maybe he thinks he needs to protect you from himself. Men doubt their worthiness all the time, and their egos have to be propped up a good bit. It seems ridiculous, but it's true. And if he's defensive about his physical disabilities, maybe it's easier to close you out than let you closer."

Now, that made sense to me. Sean had been super-sensitive about his physique, always flexing and trying to sound tough, but that aspect of his personality had just turned me off. Too much ego. There needed to be a balance between being chivalrous and courteous and being a total douche-bag.

Booker had been more than that. He'd put himself in harm's way to save me, and I could never thank him enough for that. He'd been a warrior for me when I needed one the most.

The thought made me pause. He didn't think I'd slept with him as a thank you for saving me, did he? That was ridiculous. Why couldn't I find a guy that didn't have a million hang-ups about shit?

"I don't know that it matters, Virginia, because he's been gone for the past two days. I haven't seen him or his dog at all."

The older woman waved a hand. "He'll be back. I wouldn't worry about it."

As the week stretched on, though, I began to lose hope.

8

"You have to come talk to this woman. She doesn't want to deal with me anymore."

I sighed, frustrated, as I wove through traffic. "I don't have time to talk to her. I'm on my way to a meeting to purchase a foreclosed property."

Tanner sighed on the other end of the line. "Okay, well, she said to tell you that you have an obligation to the people of the Willows, too."

I sighed. "I'll make time to stop in tomorrow."

"I'll let her know," Tanner said, before hanging up.

If I was honest, I had let my responsibility to the Willows slip over the past month. I'd put Tanner in charge of maintenance calls, basically, and just slept there occasionally. While I'd been at the Willows, I hadn't been as focused on the rest of my holdings, and that was my fault. I was supposed to have been there temporarily while I found and hired a new building manager, but it hadn't worked out that way. I'd gotten a little lazy and comfortable in the old building. It was why I'd bought it in the first place.

Hiring a new manager had become less and less pressing,

until I'd just let it go for a while. If the residents needed something fixed more than basic handiwork, I just called my guys to come work on it. I had a dedicated team that normally did the rehab work on the spaces I bought. Bill was my plumbing guy and Tanner did general construction. I had a few more guys that moved as a team from location to location.

The next property I planned to look at was in the same condition as the Willows had been, but this one housed a lot of older veterans. It was worn and tired, and the residents had been there a long time. The owners didn't have the money to refurbish with the current economy, let alone maintain. I did. This building would not be a money-maker, though. The Willows had been my first money-making aberration. This one, the Burle Building, was going to be my second. Normally I bought the buildings, rehabbed them, then sold them for a profit. The more I got to know the residents, though, the harder it was to sell. I'd been getting soft in my old age.

Something about the Willows had stuck with me, though. Maybe it had called to me because Catalina had moved in almost the same month, and I'd been reluctantly fascinated, seeing her come and go through the building. I'd even become attuned to the scent of her laundry detergent and softener.

Blue still looked for her. Every once in a while he'd let out a dramatic whine. Dobermans were known for being a little dramatic, but this was different. It was like he was missing something, or someone. Or maybe I was just anthropomorphizing.

As soon as I turned into the parking lot of the Willows the next afternoon, he knew where he was. He leaped out of the truck and ran to the front door.

Anxiety tightened my gut. I'd gotten delayed with other tasks and it was later than I expected to be here. Cat didn't seem to work nine to five, though, so there was always the chance I would see her. On the nights I stayed here, I tried to come in at odd times, when I thought she might be tucked into her apartment.

That was so lame. I was basically hiding from a woman because she was a temptation to my sanity.

I let Blue through the front door and he bolted down the hallway. I thought he was heading to the manager's apartment, but he veered left into the laundry room. I thought I heard a small scream, then him crying and whining, the same kind of excited noise he usually made when I'd been gone a couple of days. Dobies were incredibly loyal to their owners, and mourned them when they were gone or away.

When I rounded the corner, I found him on the ground trying to fit into Catalina's lap. I couldn't tell if she was laughing or crying. Had Blue knocked her down? I stepped forward to drag him away, but she wrapped her arms around his thick neck and held the dog to her.

Fuck. This was exactly what I didn't want to happen.

Cat looked up at me and her cinnamon-colored eyes were full of tears, but I wasn't sure of the reason. She swiped them away as she rubbed my traitorous dog.

"Did he hurt you?"

"No," she laughed, winking at him. "But he got pretty fresh. I was leaning over into the washer and he almost pushed me in with his hard schnoz," she gasped, laughing like I'd never seen her laugh before. Blue washed her face with his tongue as she gasped in breath, trying to push him away, giggling uncontrollably.

She was stunningly beautiful, her hair in a thick braid over her shoulder. A few curls had escaped the braid, though, framing her face, and I was reminded all over again why I wanted to kiss her. She wore no makeup, but it didn't matter. She didn't need it.

"I have to balance on the edge of the washer because I'm so

short, and he bumped me. But we're all good. I know buddy," she crooned, stroking Blue, and the dog just melted into her.

I remembered the feel of her touch very well, and I was damned close to being jealous of my dog.

Cat focused on me, the lightness in her expression fading as she looked me up and down. "How are you, Booker? How's your hand?"

"I'm fine," I said, voice gruff. I splayed my fingers and showed her my palm. The cut had aggravated me for about a week, then I'd pulled the stitches and it had faded away. Same with the abs, but she didn't request to see those. I would have stripped naked and walked over glass to her if I could bring that happiness into her expression again.

And as I looked at her, I noticed dark circles beneath her eyes. "Are you okay?"

She nodded. "I'm fine," she said, but he could tell there was more to it she wasn't saying. Something was off, but I certainly wasn't in a position to demand answers from her.

"I, uh, should probably get going. You need help with your laundry? Did you reach everything?"

When I upgraded the appliances, I hadn't taken into account shorter people having issues with the bigger, heavier duty machines. I moved to the washer and leaned down inside, pulling out a few pieces of silky, crumpled fabric. Oh, shit. These were panties. Arousal snapped down through my gut and I tossed the tiny little garments into the dryer before I was tempted to shake them out and look at them.

"Thank you," Cat said, climbing to her feet. Blue continued to lean into her, and I was surprised at the ease with which he'd accepted her again. The dog was naturally standoffish and leery of people, but something about Catalina made him happy and relaxed.

Just like it had me.

Slamming the door shut on the dryer, I turned the dial and pressed the button. Even the dryer controls were probably a reach for her. I'd call one of the guys to run a stool over, or figure something out. Maybe a step along the length of the machines.

"Thank you," Cat said, setting her laundry basket in front of the dryer. "I'll come back and get it in a little while."

We stared at each other for a minute before I stepped back to let her pass. She paused in front of me and looked up. She rested a palm on my cheek. "I'm glad you're doing okay, Booker. I was worried about you."

Before I could come up with a response, she'd turned and left the laundry room. I grabbed Blue's collar before he took off after her. "Hold," I murmured.

It didn't feel right, letting her go without some kind of good-bye. Should I have kissed her or something? I felt like I needed to tell her how shitty the month had been since I'd been with her.

We weren't in that kind of space, though. Yes, we'd had a good time, but we were on different trajectories. The Willows had been a place to pause and catch my breath. I just hadn't left yet.

I went to the manager's apartment and set Blue up with a Kong loaded with peanut butter and treats. He would be through it in less that half an hour, but it would give me time to go talk to Virginia. She'd been persistent with Tanner, pretty much demanding my presence yesterday, so I'd better see what she was upset about.

When she opened the door at my knock, I expected a hello.

"It's about damn time," Virginia snapped, shocking me. I'd never heard her cuss. "Where have you been?"

I didn't appreciate the invasiveness of the question, but I remembered that Virginia had always been a good friend here. "I have responsibilities other than the Willows. What's wrong?"

Virginia moved to the living room and sat in her favorite chair. I perched on the edge of the couch and waited for her to tell me what she was upset about.

"I thought you liked Catalina," she said, her gaze probing.

I sighed. I should have known she'd be after me about this. "I do like Catalina, Mrs. Virginia. She's a strong, beautiful girl."

The old woman leaned in. "You two hooked up, didn't you?"

My jaw clamped. "Did Cat tell you that?"

"Not in so many words. I can tell something is in the air, though. She dances around any questions I have and finds something else to do. I might be old, but I can see heartbreak."

I rocked back. Heartbreak? We hadn't even been with each other more than a day. How could I have broken her heart? "I think you're wrong, Virginia. I helped her out of a bad situation and she feels indebted to me. I didn't break her heart."

Virginia's eyes narrowed. "So, you think she slept with you because she felt indebted?"

I winced. "No, I don't think that at all. I don't know why she slept with me. I think it was an aberration on both of our parts."

Virginia shook her head. "Do you regret it?"

"No," I said, and it was definitive. I would never regret being with her. I would carry the memory of it in my heart.

"Why won't you be with her?"

I stood to pace to the wall of windows. I looked out on the courtyard. Virginia could see a lot here, more than I realized. She probably saw me every time I took Blue out.

"Catalina has a beautiful soul," I told her eventually. "She deserves someone better than me."

"Like Tanner."

I glanced at her incredulously. "Tanner? She's not dating Tanner, is she? Has she lost her damn mind?"

Virginia grinned and shook her head. "No, she's not dating

Tanner, but he's the only one around now that would be able to help her."

"Help her with what?" I turned to face the woman.

She looked down at her clasped hands. "She asked me to keep it a secret, so I can't say anything. Just know that it would behoove you to start spending some time around here again."

I sighed, hating the secrecy. "I'm not the guy for her, Virginia. I have too many ghosts in my closet. She doesn't deserve to be saddled with my issues."

"Did you talk to her about them? Maybe they aren't as big to her as they are to you."

I sighed, grim. Waking up that morning a month ago and feeling the anger coursing through me, looking for an outlet, I knew I couldn't stay next to her a moment longer. The anger was unpredictable and sometimes volatile, and very rarely had a focus. I knew it came from frustration with what had happened in Afghanistan, but I was still learning to get rid of the anger. Blue helped. He seemed to sense when my emotions were getting the best of me and would plant himself against my legs. He'd not been trained in veteran-specific service dog work, but he did a good job for me. "She has her own life to deal with," I said eventually.

Her lips pursing, she shook her head at me and I could tell she was frustrated, but I didn't know what to say. Catalina would be better off without me. Period.

"Go talk to her."

"I just did," I said, exasperated. "In the laundry room."

Virginia leaned forward. "And you didn't notice anything? You didn't see the bags under her eyes?"

I scowled. I had seen them, damn it. "What's wrong with her?"

The old woman clamped her mouth shut. "It's not a what. It's a who. That's all I'm saying."

Sean. Why hadn't I asked her about him? Had something happened? Was he out of jail?

"Why wouldn't she have told me?"

"You told her it wasn't going any further, so why would she burden you?"

I grimaced, hating to have my words returned to me.

"I'll go talk to her," I promised.

Virginia gave me a nod. "I thought you would. Tell her not to be mad at me."

I left the apartment feeling like I'd been shanghaied by an eighty-year-old woman. I also knew she only had Catalina's interests at heart. And mine, as well, to an extent. If something was going on with Catalina, I felt like I needed to know.

I had no business trying to pin her down on anything, though. Maybe... maybe we just needed proximity and she would talk to me. To that end, I went downstairs and listened for the buzzer on the dryer. And she loved Blue, so I would take him with me when I delivered her clothes.

Everything went according to plan. The buzzer went off and I loaded up her laundry basket. I didn't fold the clothes. That seemed too personal. Then my dog and I headed upstairs, basket in tow.

When she answered the door, Cat looked at me like I was a crazy person. "I was coming back down for it."

"I know. I just thought I would help you out."

She stared at me for a long minute, and I figured her bullshit meter was pegged. She didn't really say anything, though. Blue slipped into her apartment, sleek and muscular. Sighing, she stepped back and waved me in. "Just set it on the coffee table, if you would."

I did as I was told and set it down. Cat sat in the chair and started folding. Blue plopped down beside her and stretched out on the floor, seemingly well at home. I didn't understand that dog. He was so particular about so many things, but he worshipped the ground this woman walked on. "Can I help you?"

Again, she gave him a strange look. "Sure..."

Silently, they began folding clothes. I was okay with the t-shirts and leggings, but when we got to the bottom of the basket and the panties, I hesitated.

"We've had sex," she murmured. "I don't think there's anything in here you haven't seen."

Yes, that was true.

"I haven't seen you for a few weeks."

Yeah, I'd known this was coming. "I've been checking out my other properties."

"What other properties?" She narrowed her eyes at me. "I thought you were a maintenance man?"

"I am, often. I buy a property and go in and renovate it, make it nicer, then I sell it. Generally, that's what I do. For some reason, I've kept the Willows."

She blinked, shaking her head slightly. "So, you own the Willows."

"Yes," I admitted. "I have for about seven months. It was struggling. The owners were, rather. I came in, renovated a lot of it and moved into the Manager's office to keep an eye on things and hire a new manager. I usually move on to the next property, but I liked the feel of the building, and the residents."

"Wow," she breathed, and I could tell she wasn't sure what to do with the information. I hadn't really planned on telling her about it, but I thought I should open up a little since I was expecting her to do the same.

"And Tanner and Bill..."

"Work on my renovation crew."

"So, why are you telling me this?" She crossed her arms over her breasts, almost defensively. "Am I supposed to appreciate the attention you pay me now that I know you're the owner?"

I rocked back in the seat. "What? Why the hell would you say that? No, I don't want you to appreciate the attention. I was trying to connect, or something. I don't fucking know." I pushed up from the chair, frustrated and not sure how to deal with it. "Come on, Blue."

The dog climbed reluctantly to his feet and followed me to the door. My hand was on the knob when Cat huffed out a breath. "Wait, Booker. I'm sorry."

I glanced at her as she stopped beside me, her hand on my arm. "I guess I'm waiting for your asshole side to show. I apologize if I misread your intentions."

"You did," I growled, wondering what the hell I was even doing here. I'd told her I didn't want a relationship, yet here I was, coming back for more because of some vague warning from a neighbor.

"Come back in, then, and hang out for a little bit. I have a roast in the oven Blue can help me eat."

The dog lifted his head at his name and she snorted. "Typical male."

It was titillating and yet strange to have Booker in the apartment. Worrisome. I was frazzled enough without having to entertain him. If it was just me, I'd be in sleep pants and a T-shirt, folded into my computer chair working on a project. Now, though, I felt like I needed to engage, though he'd shut me down.

Walking this line was going to kill me.

"If you'll excuse me a minute," I murmured, grabbing the

laundry basket. "I'll change my clothes and get something going to have with the roast."

I hustled out of the living room, feeling the weight of his gaze on my back. Or maybe he was watching my ass. Even though he'd said that there would be nothing else between us, I could tell by the way he looked at me that there could still be. What would he do if I walked out of the bedroom naked?

I wasn't going to try that.

Maybe we just needed to know each other better. The fact that he'd opened up about owning the Willows indicated he might be open to that as well.

I changed clothes and walked back into the kitchen. The pork roast could be taken out any time. There were potatoes, onions and carrots in the pan with it, but there needed to be something else. I ripped open a can of biscuits and punched the seam to pop the tube, then I placed them on a cookie sheet. I pulled the roast out and put the biscuits in. Twenty minutes.

Two years ago Mom and I had made apple butter. A jar of that as a side with the biscuits and pork would be perfection. I set it out on the counter seating area, then gathered plates and silverware. We could eat in the dining room area, but I liked this counter. It seemed homier to me.

"Can I get you a beer? Or a soda?" I peered over toward the couch where Booker was sitting.

"Ice water, please."

That was unexpected. Most guys I knew would have gone for the beer. Booker had proven over and over again, though, that he wasn't most men. And I felt bad because I was holding him to a standard that other men had created. I needed to quit doing that.

I also needed to let him know what was going on, but I didn't want to look like I was a damn damsel in distress. I was a strong, competent woman making my way through life. I had a thriving business and some money in the bank. But I was a little out of my depth.

This could be where his military experience might come in handy.

I went out to the living room and sank down onto the couch beside him, curling my feet beneath me. "So, how did you get into owning properties?"

He smiled a little and cleared his throat. "My grandmother gave me a small trust when I turned twenty-one. I didn't touch it until I got out of the Army. By then it was a decent little egg. I didn't want to just buy a house and be done. I wanted to build onto what I already had, so I looked at investment properties. I bought a good sized, rundown house, renovated it and lost my ass." He grinned, his fingers tapping on the back of the couch. "But I learned a ton. So, the next one I bought was a lot smaller, but it needed more work. I took the time and did most of it myself, and sold it for about double what I put in it."

"Nice," I breathed. "That's impressive."

It was also impressive that his face had lightened. It looked like he loved doing this.

"Once I thought could be a fluke. But I bought a second house and did the same thing. Then a third. Then I bought my first apartment building. And I put higher quality materials into it. It sold before I was even finished." He shrugged, lightly. "That was about five years ago. I've been going on ever since."

"That's really cool," I told him, and it was. "I'd like to do something like that someday. My papa and I used to build things together, and I loved it."

"You should. It's very satisfying. Is he still around?"

"Yes, he lives with my mother over toward Dayton. I see them every couple of weeks. Someone offers up a house and we have dinner together. And of course birthdays and holidays. My dad is a retired truck driver, and they still take off on excursions just so he can be on the road."

Booker smirked. "I can understand that. I love to drive. When I got out of the Army I took a couple of months to decide what I thought I wanted to do, and where."

"Is your family from here?" I couldn't remember him ever speaking about them.

"Nah. Most of my family is from up around Chicago. My grandmother was from this area, though, and she always told me how much she loved it. The economy was growing at the time and I thought I could make money, so I settled here."

I shook my head. "It's crazy to me that you own this building."

"It's best if I blend in when I take over the properties. People aren't always happy with change, even if it's for the better."

"I can understand that."

We talked for a few more minutes about other buildings he'd renovated, until the buzzer went off on the oven. "The biscuits are ready," I told him. "Come have a seat."

I removed the biscuits and put them in a little towel-draped basket. The roast was still steaming hot, so I just set everything in front of our plates and started dishing things out.

The roast was phenomenal. There was just enough thyme and garlic on the bark. The carrots were cooked perfectly, and when Booker spread the apple butter on the biscuit, he groaned out loud.

"This was amazing," he said, leaning back on the stool. "I feel like my gut is going to bust."

"Don't do that," I laughed. "We just got you stitched up."

He gave me a funny sideways grin. "Isn't that the truth?"

Leaning over, I fed Blue a piece of the tender fat. The dog gobbled it up without even tasting it, making me laugh.

"I want to thank you for tonight," Booker said. "I know we kind of took a step back, but I appreciate the lack of animosity."

I shrugged, trying to appear nonchalant. "What is there to be upset about? You stated your preferences and I think it's smart to take a step back. We were caught up in the moment. I've learned more about you tonight than I ever have before. We weren't ready for the physical part. Yes, it was amazing, but I don't normally jump into bed for a one-night stand."

Booker grimaced, like he didn't appreciate being labelled that way. Yes, we'd had sex twice, but I still considered it a one-night stand. Maybe now that we knew each other it could be upgraded to a friends-with-benefits type situation.

The change in distinction opened up the possibility that it might happen again. A thrill went through me at the thought, and I tried to maintain my composure. He was within two feet, though... New topic.

"So, tell me about the Rangers. Do you miss it?"

"Every single day," Booker said, sighing.

I turned to face him. "It seems like I remember seeing an article about a serviceman with an amputation returning to active duty."

"It is possible," he admitted, "but I didn't feel like I would be the best, physically, for my men. You have to know that you can rely on your teammate in any situation, and as you saw when Sean kicked my ankle, the prosthetic isn't perfect."

"That could have happened to your regular leg, though, too."

"Granted, but I didn't feel comfortable staying in at less than perfect ability."

I nodded, understanding the drive for perfection. Now that I was on my own, my projects had to be creative and timely, and satisfy the customer so that I had repeat business. I loved what I did, but I had to approach it as a business and not as a hobby like I used to.

"The average person changes jobs seven times in their lifetime."

He laughed a little. "I think I've done more than that already."

"I think it's good to change things up. Keeps you on your toes and interested in life."

"Maybe," he murmured.

The silence stretched a little, but it wasn't awkward. Eventually I slid off the stool and started gathering dirty dishes. Booker immediately slid off his own stool to help me. He moved to the sink and began running hot water. "Have you heard from Sean?"

I glanced at him. That had been very slick. "Not directly. Any chance you have cameras up in the building anywhere?"

Booker looked at me sharply. "What's been going on?"

I made a face as I retrieved a fresh dish towel. "Not sure. Just a few odd things. Lights out outside. Hang up calls on my cell from out of state. There was a dead cat positioned under the wheel of my car the other day, and I know for a fact I didn't hit it."

Booker turned off the water and leaned against the sink. "What does your gut tell you?"

My gut was churning right now. And it was telling me I was being messed with. "I think Sean was extremely pissed when things didn't go his way, and I think he'll try to get back at me any way he can."

I must have looked like I needed a hug, because he drew me into his arms. For a long moment I sagged into him, loving the feel of the heat of his body against mine. It made everything I'd been dealing with over the past month fade away. Yes, I was strong, but it was nice being not strong sometimes, and letting another bear the weight.

Booker was more than capable. His strong arms wrapped

around me, and he pulled me between his spread legs. Turning my head, I rested it against the shelf of his pectorals.

"There are a couple of security cameras outside, and I know the building next to us has a couple. Let me look back through and see if anything popped up."

"Okay," I murmured, and I forced myself to pull back.

His arms didn't want to release me. I took that as a good sign. I hated that he finally did let me go.

This was such a weird position to be in. I mean, we'd already fucked, but it was almost like we were starting over and introducing ourselves. I didn't hold out any hope that his expectations had changed, or anything. Booker had said he wasn't interested in any kind of relationship, so that's what I was going on. To avoid heartbreak, I would have to be more circumspect as well.

No expectations meant no disappointment.

9

I went down to the apartment and my laptop, and started pulling surveillance footage. The two cameras at the Willows were old and grainy. They'd been on the building a long time, and never updated. I should have updated them when I first bought the building.

I waited for the download server to open. It was as clunky as the camera feeds were. It took a while to find the correct feed. I could only scan a day at a time, so I started with the day he attacked Catalina. It was easy enough to remember because of the date of my hospital admission.

I'd looked at this day before to see if I could see Sean, but he hadn't appeared in either of the cameras. It seemed like he had avoided them deliberately. Probably because he knew he was going to assault Cat and he didn't want any record of it.

One camera looked out over the small back parking lot. It was only big enough for about twenty cars. The rest of the residents had to park on the street.

The second camera looked down onto the front door, but it was positioned badly. It caught people from the back as they entered the building, and only caught their partial faces if they left the same way. Most exited through the back door, which required a key to get into.

This all needed to change, I fumed as I went through days upon days of residents entering the building. Then there were the pizza delivery people, the Amazon drivers, the UPS. Our mail was delivered by a muscular blonde woman. It usually took her about four minutes to fill the boxes, then she left the same way.

It was about two weeks in when I saw a man I didn't recognize. Tall and bald, he walked up to the door and peered in through the glass, then he pulled it open and went inside. I spotted him again a few days later. When I looked at the parking lot footage, I saw him in the rear lot wandering between the cars. It was obvious he wasn't a resident.

Okay, now we were getting somewhere. I took a screenshot of one of the frames and printed it off. It wasn't perfect, but I could see a little bit of his face in this one. I put the picture aside and continued screening. By the time I got to today's footage, it was after midnight. It didn't matter, though. I had three pictures of men I didn't know in the stack. I also had a picture of one of the men carrying a black trash bag, then leaning over beside Cat's Toyota. The next morning she'd gone out and spotted the dead cat. It was obvious from her reaction. She cupped a hand over her mouth and backed away. One of the elderly neighbors came out a little later and disposed of the animal.

It was after two by the time I went to bed, but I felt like I had an idea of who was wreaking havoc. I had a list of things to do tomorrow, but first thing, I was having Tanner mount more cameras.

The next morning I mounted a small camera directly on the door frame to the entrance of the building. It wasn't very big, but it had come well-reviewed. This particular model was motion activated and could be watched on a smart phone. The picture was incredible.

Tanner arrived a little after noon with a couple of the other crew and they brought boxes of equipment with them. They started by mounting a camera at every corner of the building, then two more in the back lot. I knew the bill for this would be significant, but I didn't care.

Last night, being with Catalina, it had been exhilarating and humbling at the same time. I'd basically told her I was a dead end relationship, but she still talked to me like we could be friends. I wished I could be more for her.

Last night, after watching hours of surveillance, I'd dreamed of basically the same thing, but there had been a more ominous tone to the footage reeling through my head. I could tell the footage was building to something, but I was unable to get out of it.

I'd woken angry, fists clenched and a scream caught in my throat as I'd looked down at Catalina's lifeless body.

That's what my mind did to me. It rearranged history for the worst possible outcome. I knew Catalina was safe upstairs, but I worried and replayed what happened repeatedly. And that worry coalesced into anxiety and night terrors. After the attack she'd been through, I was sure she'd love to wake up to me looming over her in attack mode.

It had been hard to walk away last night, because my body still craved her. I refused to let my body and my libido control my life, though, and put Cat in danger.

It was after lunchtime by the time I headed up to Virginia's, pictures in my hands. When I'd spoken to Roger Miller, the building owner to the rear of the Willows, he'd immediately scoured his security footage as well. And he'd come up with the same three men as I had in my hand. Virginia was my secondary layer of security, and if she didn't know any of them we would be in trouble.

It took her a minute to answer my knock, and she seemed a little surprised to see me. But when I asked for her advice, she perked up with pride.

"I need to know if you know these three men."

I handed her the three pictures I had printed off, as well as the pics Roger had printed off. Shuffling to the chair she preferred, she fumbled for her glasses as she sat down.

Virginia pursed her lips as she looked at the first man. There were three different pictures of him and she spread them out on the arm of the couch, to her right. Then she held up the second man's picture. "This is Mr. Nguyen's grandson. He recently started school at Ohio State. I don't remember his name. I'm sorry."

Cool. That reduced the pool of suspects to two.

She held up one of the last man's pictures, the bald guy. "He looks familiar to me but I'm not sure why."

Leaning over, she looked at the pictures spread on the couch arm. "I don't know about this one..."

The guy had dark hair clipped close to his head and dark eyes. He wore what appeared to be a running jacket in each photo. This was the one I thought left the dead cat under Catalina's vehicle. It was gratifying that she didn't know him, and made me even more suspicious.

Virginia was looking at the first man again. "You know, do you mind if I call someone down?"

"No, that's fine. Call who you need to."

She dialed her ancient cordless phone. Did she even have a cell phone?

"He'll be down in a few minutes," she said when she hung up. "Can I get you a glass of tea?"

"Sure," I said, sinking down onto the couch. I'd been so

involved in this that I hadn't had a chance to eat or drink a lot of anything, so I took the glass with appreciation. "Thank you very much."

"Obviously, you talked to Catalina. I think that man hired someone to harass her."

I sighed. "Yeah, I think you're right. I'm trying to prove it."

"Is that why there are cute boys running all over the building carrying boxes?"

I snorted. "Yes, ma'am. We're putting up cameras. These ones have been here as long as the building has, I think."

Virginia laughed. "They're not that old. It's smart, though, you wanting to take care of Catalina."

I went still. "This is for everyone, not just Catalina."

Virginia waved a hand. "Oh, I know, but it's still sweet. No one ever did anything before, so I appreciate it as well. Besides, they're fun to look at."

I snorted. Yeah, I supposed they weren't too bad looking. Two of the men on the crew were already married, though. I drank my tea, letting her ramble on about her former husband. Many years ago he'd been the building manager, but he'd gotten cancer and passed on. She'd moved upstairs and been here ever since.

Virginia was a good-hearted lady. "You need to come to the party tonight," she told him.

Ugh... was it Friday already? "I don't know. I've got a lot of work to do."

"The Vixen has been focusing on the military this month. You should tune in. It might be enlightening."

"I'll think about it."

I really wouldn't, but I would never tell her that.

There was a knock on the door and Virginia pushed up out of her chair. When she came back she was walking with the resident from 6D, I thought. He was a quiet man, a writer I think I'd heard.

"Killian, do you know either of these men?"

Virginia held up the papers and he focused on the bald man. A sly grin crossed his lips. "Yes, ma'am. That's Miss Angelique's masseuse."

I blinked. Okay, that's not what I'd been expecting. "Really?"

Killian nodded. "Oh, yes, I remember that bald head. They get very... noisy while he's rubbing her down."

I choked out a laugh. Fuck... "You're positive?"

Killian nodded his graying head. "Absolutely. I ran into him in the elevator once and he walked right past my door to knock on Angelique's. He was there for about an hour and I heard him leave about an hour later."

Virginia nodded. "I knew I'd seen him in the building for some reason, but couldn't remember why. Thank you, Killian. Can you keep track of when you see him?"

"It's usually every Wednesday."

I needed to check the dates on these pics. I bet they would match up. Killian seemed very sure.

"Okay, you guys have helped me a lot. I'm going to go see if Catalina recognizes this one, then."

"Is everyone okay? Is there anything we need to know about?" Killian asked.

"I'll tell you later, Killian," Virginia said, escorting him to the door. "Right now it needs to stay quiet, and you're always on that face book thing."

"I can keep a secret, Virginia," he protested, but she shooed him out anyway.

I carried my glass into the kitchen and set it in the sink. Then I headed out, catching her in the hallway. "I'm going to go, too, and talk to Catalina. Thank you for your help."

"How will you figure out who the man is?"

"I have a couple of options," I said, grinning at her. "We'll figure out what's going on."

"I'm so glad Catalina has you on her side, Booker."

I blinked and gave her a lopsided smile. Then I leaned down and gave her a kiss on the cheek. "She's lucky to have you, as well."

Virginia blushed and swatted my shoulder. "Oh, you. Go share some of that charm with your girl."

I didn't argue.

BOOKER STOOD ON MY DOORSTEP, looking more delicious than any man had a right to be. It looked like he hadn't shaved in a day or so, the lean skin of his cheeks bristly with hair. Normally, he had a light mustache and chin beard of hair a shade darker than that on his head. His eyes seemed tired to me, though they were lit with some inner excitement right now.

He lifted his head when he entered the apartment. "Something smells good."

I grinned at him. A man could always be wooed by appealing to his stomach. But it was the rest of the stuff that had to keep him around. "I'm making some appetizers for the Love Vixen listen party."

Booker didn't literally roll his eyes, but it was there in his silence. He gave me a bland smile, making me laugh. "Oh, whatever. I've caught you listening to it, too."

"I might have caught the end of a military program," he admitted.

"There's another one tonight."

"I know," he sighed dramatically. "Virginia told me."

I grinned and led him into the living room. "What's she up to, today?"

"Helping me play detective," he said, pulling out a few papers. There were pictures of men on them. He held one out and I took the paper.

"Do you recognize this guy?"

I frowned as I looked down at the not-so-clear face. "Not really."

He handed me another paper. It appeared to be the same man carrying a bag and leaning over in the parking lot. I recognized my car. "Is he the one that put the cat under my wheel?"

"It appears to be."

I looked at the papers again, but he didn't look familiar. "I don't know, Booker. If I've seen him I don't recognize him."

Booker frowned. "Okay. Well, I don't know if you've been out or not today, but I'm having some guys put up some cameras around the building."

I nodded. "Tanner was here earlier. There's one at the end of my hallway basically looking at my door."

He nodded. "Yes, I told them to put it there. And if I can have your permission, I'd like to give you a Ring."

My heart stopped in my chest. Wait, what?

"You can mount it easily to the doorjamb and as soon as it catches movement it alerts you," he continued.

My heart fell. A Ring. One of those doorbell things. I had to turn away for a minute, peering in through the kitchen doorway like I was worried about the food in the oven. I wasn't, but it gave me a chance to collect my face. "Okay," I said, turning back to him. "That might come in handy. If I had seen Sean, there, I probably could have been more prepared. And this entire mess could have been avoided."

"Possibly," he admitted. "But more than likely he would have come after you a different way. Where does he stand with his charges?"

"He pleaded not guilty, of course. I spoke to a lawyer, though, and she said it's a ploy to get the charges withdrawn or dismissed. They should be contacting you about your statement on the off chance it actually goes to court. He's still in jail and she doesn't seem to think he's going anywhere because he doesn't have the money to post bond. The judge was not happy that he struck the arresting officer, so it's pretty high."

Booker snorted. "Yeah, I'm sure he doesn't want him on the streets."

I motioned for Booker to sit on the couch, and I sat down beside him. Close, but not too close. My heart was still beating out of my chest though. He just looked so good, even tired and a little grizzled. "So, how do we figure out who this guy is?"

Booker stretched an arm along the back of the couch. "Well, I'm not positive, but I would hope that if we see him touch something we can get the PD to collect a print and run it. However they do that kind of thing. Since you already have a criminal case running..."

"Not with this guy, though," I interrupted.

"No, but that shouldn't matter. You might think about going ahead and filing a police report just to get it down on paper. CYA."

"What's that?"

"Cover your ass. Do whatever you need to do to prove you're not the one in the wrong. Create a paper trail."

"Yeah," I sighed. "Makes sense."

I did not want to call the police again. It was probably prudent, though.

"And if the police decide it's not worth their time?"

"Then I know a guy that can probably help. His son is a private investigator at a firm downtown. We might be able to get him to work some magic."

This had become so complicated and drawn out. Seven months ago I was just a young woman living it up with my best friend, drinking too much and not working as hard as I should have been. Now I was responsible for my life and had a growing business. And I was learning about all these fun things like police reports and stalkers.

The silence must have gone on too long because Booker squeezed my shoulder. "It will be okay, Cat. I promise."

I nodded, his gentle touch weakening my foundations. I wanted to crawl into his lap and bawl my eyes out, but I knew he wouldn't respect that. Besides, what I was dealing with nothing compared to what he'd gone through. Deployments and terrifying injuries... yeah, no comparison.

"You know, you're going above and beyond for me," I said finally. "And I don't understand why."

He blinked and frowned, his solid brows dropping down to shadow his brilliant eyes. "Real men don't behave this way. They don't need to."

"How should they behave?" I asked curiously, my heart damn near aching out of my chest.

"With honor in all things," he said immediately.

I could tell he meant it, too. I would love to have another chance with Booker. I wouldn't push, though. He had to want to be with me.

"What is your first name?" I asked, curious. I'd wondered before, but never had a chance to ask him.

Narrowing his eyes, he pursed his lips. "I don't know if I can trust you with that information."

I laughed, incredulous. "Okay. Not like you don't know everything about me, or anything..."

I moved to get up. The appetizers needed to be checked, anyway.

"Don't get all huffy," he said, holding out his hand for me to stop. "I'm just teasing. It's Gabriel."

Oh, wow... that suited him so perfectly. A warrior angel.

"Thank you for sharing," I told him solemnly. "I still need to check on my appetizers."

Gabriel pulled his hand away and made a flourish as he gave me room to get by. Impulsively, I leaned down and pressed a kiss to his forehead. "I love your name."

I did. It suited him so well. He probably didn't see himself as the hero I did, but it didn't matter.

The apps were fine, they just needed a few more minutes. I glanced at the clock. I needed to get to Virginia's in about an hour. I had just enough time to shower and get ready.

Did I want to call the cops now to file a report? Not really.

"I'll get out of here," Booker said from behind me. "I know you have stuff to do."

"I do, yes," I admitted. "I think I'll file the police report after I go to Virginia's."

"That should be fine. I'll see if I can get in touch with my buddy. It can't hurt to feel him out about what needs done."

I followed him as he walked to the door and let himself out. I wanted to lean up and kiss him or something, but I held onto the door instead. "Thank you, Booker, for everything. On the one hand, I wish Virginia hadn't said anything to you, but I do appreciate your help with this. You've done a lot of research and I can't even imagine what all these cameras are costing you."

He shrugged and looked down the hallway at the newly mounted camera. "Doesn't matter. You have a right to feel safe in your home."

Once again tears pressed at my eyelids and I nodded, mouth tight. Booker drew me into his arms and hugged me close. "You'll be okay. We'll get these assholes."

I nodded against his chest and rested my hands on his sides, breathing him in. "I know."

I wanted more, though. I wanted to know that I could see him after everything was done. I doubted he would offer that, though. I would have to convince him he had worth to me for more than dealing with the emergency.

I pulled away, already thinking about how I could entice him to be with me. Maybe I should write the Love Vixen.

Oh... the thought definitely had merit. I would have to figure out how to do it, and when. Feeling lighter inside than I had for a month, I gave him a grin. "I'll see you later. Gabriel."

He winced as he turned away. "I knew I shouldn't have told you..."

I laughed as he disappeared down the hallway.

10

I'd barely sat down in my recliner when there was a knock at my door. Sighing, I looked for the T-shirt I'd gotten out of the closet, but I didn't see it. "Where'd my shirt go?" I asked Blue.

The dog cocked his head at me, but didn't respond. Then he turned his head and raced to the door, whining. Ah, must be Cat.

I swung the door open, holding Blue with the opposite hand. Cat stood on the other side of the door, a smile ready on her face. It faded as she caught sight of me in my towel. Her eyes drifted down my body, lingering, and I started to respond. It was what happened when a beautiful woman looked at a hungry man like that.

She blinked and jerked, her pale cheeks flushing. She held a plate out to me. "I know you won't come to the party, but I thought you would like some snacks when you listen to the Vixen. Grilled chicken skewers, some pot stickers, smashed potatoes and a couple of brownies."

It was my turn to shift uncomfortably, because yes, the Love Vixen was playing in the background. She grinned at me as I took the plate, sniffing appreciatively. Blue took that moment to pull away from me and lunge at Cat. I jerked forward to catch him, still holding the plate, and I felt the towel loosen from around my hips. There was no way I could grab it, so I just stood there, in all my bare-assed glory. I thought she'd focus on the white shower prosthetic I wore, but she barely glanced at it before focusing on other things. Or, *one* other thing.

She finally looked away to greet Blue, laughing as he jumped around her like he was on springs. I bent down to retrieve the towel, but I didn't cover myself. She'd already seen everything there was to see, so whatever. "Thank you for the food. I appreciate it."

Cat grinned at him, her eyes steady on my face. "No problem. I know you like food."

"I do, and if you made it, I know I'll love it."

Her smile broadened, but she didn't say anything more. Blue rubbed against her thigh, looking up at her like the drama-dick he was. Cat rubbed him all over and it was obvious she was really trying not to look at my erection, which had not gone down in spite of the cool air. Relief was mere feet away, and he knew it.

"Would you like to come in?" I asked her, hoping more than I had in a long time.

She blushed furiously, then met his gaze. There was sadness there now. "As much as I would love to, I don't think it's a good idea. Not if we're not going to continue as friends. I'm already having issues keeping you at a distance and honoring your wishes."

I rocked back, hurt and a little angry. I didn't have anyone to blame but myself, though. I'd drawn the line and now I was trying to tease her over it. "You're completely right. My apologies."

I covered myself with the towel. Cat reached out to touch my upper arm, and I looked at her.

"If you change your mind about exploring more than friendship, please let me know. I think we could be exceptional together."

My throat went tight at the possibility of calling her mine. And loving her whenever I wanted. Being the one she relied upon all the time.

"You don't want this broken down wreck," I whispered, my throat raw.

She sighed, and began to turn away. "You know, you keep telling me that, but I think you're the one that's afraid."

With that, she gave Blue a last pat and turned away. I didn't say anything as she left me standing there in the hallway. I knew she was probably right. I didn't like it though.

"Come on, Blue."

~

DEAR LOVE VIXEN,

Damn this is hard. I'm a retired SEAL. My last mission was difficult. I've..... come home with scars inside and out. I'm a big guy 6'6",lol. Some say well-built, and not bad looking. I like my women to be more than a hand full in all body parts. A full-figured woman. Every time I approach one they think I'm joking, that I'm making fun of them. I've seen this girl at the local coffee shop. She comes in shy and quiet orders her caramel latte no whip, gets her potato soup and goes to a secluded table. She pulls out a book. Yep. Military Romance..... I looked it up. I really want to get to know her, ask her out, but don't want the usual to happen. She looks like she's had a lot of pain in her life. It's in her eyes. She pulls me in... Okay, enough. You get the idea. My buddy's girl suggested I ask you how to approach her, so hell, here I am asking.

Big Bear in Boise

Aw. My heart ached for the big bear guy. It had to be hard coming home damaged. I wondered if his wounds were visible or not. Booker looked gorgeous, but he'd received a terrible disability. Looking at him, you noticed nothing, even when he walked. I wouldn't have even known about the amputation if it hadn't been for him being attacked that night and taking the leg off when he went to bed. His voice, when he chose to speak, was the only indication that he'd been hurt.

It didn't bother me, but I wondered if he thought he was deficient. Men, even quiet and reserved ones, still had ego issues, and this wasn't something I'd ever dealt with before.

As if she'd heard my thoughts, Virginia leaned over. "I think you should write the Vixen. Maybe she has some insight into their minds. What do you think?"

It was not a crazy idea. I'd had it myself. "I doubt I would get through."

Virginia shrugged. "Might be worth trying."

Her words stuck with me all that night and into the next day.

"What the hell," I said, pulling up my writing app. I pounded out a letter, then went back through and changed some things up. Then I looked up The Love Vixen's website and went through the submission portal. Before I could second-guess myself, I hit submit.

Then I had an attack of nerves. What if he did hear my letter being read? Would he understand it was about him? *Well, yeah, dipshit, you put his name in there.*

I put it out of my mind. I had other things to think about.

I filed the second police report, though the cop looked at me like it was going to be a stretch. "Listen," I told him. "I just want it down that strange things have been happening, and if this guy is connected to my ex-boyfriend, I want it logged. Because I'm going to make sure he stays in jail as long as possible."

I handed over the copies of the photos for him to add to the report. "If nothing happens, great, but if it escalates, I've done my due diligence in informing you."

"I suggest you not take matters into your own hands, ma'am," the officer said, sounding tired.

I was getting pissed. "You know, if I had waited for cops that night, I would probably be in the hospital or dead. My building manager, an Army Ranger, kicked his ass that night, and he's the one you're going to have to worry about."

The officer's interest sharpened. "An Army Ranger, huh? My brother was a Ranger. You probably won't even need us."

I grinned, glad to see that the indifferent shell had cracked. "Maybe," I said as I walked him out.

That was done. Now I supposed I just needed to hang out and be stalked some more. Fuck...

I wanted to talk to Evie or my parents, but I didn't want to burden them with worry they didn't need.

Nothing happened for about three days. I gave Booker the space he needed, but it was hard. Other than the dramatic ex-boyfriend, there should be nothing keeping us apart. I didn't receive any notifications on the new doorbell Tanner installed, so Booker hadn't come up to see me at all. I knew he was in the building, though. Virginia called and I stopped down once to see her, but she had talked to him every day.

It was a little ridiculous, the way he was avoiding me.

When I complained to Virginia, she gave me this smug smile. "It means he's struggling."

"What do you mean?"

"I mean," she said patiently, "when a man is presented with an impossible dream, sometimes he can't believe it's for him.

Maybe he's been told all his life that certain things aren't for him. He has to decide to grab it on his own. And sometimes the woman has to prop that ego up again and again, and convince him he's the one for her."

I sighed. That meant putting my heart out there and risking it all over again. I'd done this before and it hadn't turned out well. In college, I thought I'd fallen in love. We were both artists and free spirits. We'd been together for about six months when I found out he was sharing his spirit with everyone who would take it.

I hadn't been in love with Sean, nowhere close, but I'd been hoping. I believed in the complete fairytale, though. I'd seen my parent's interactions, and I knew it was possible to find your soulmate in the middle of everyday life. My father stopped to help my mother on the interstate years ago, and that led to a thirty-plus year marriage.

I wanted that reliability, and that intimacy that only one other person in the world could give.

I felt like I'd found my person, so how did I convince him of that?

I left Virginia's feeling a little put out. Why did men have to be so pig-headed and honorable?

I ran downstairs to get my mail, but there was nothing in the box. I hoped to see Booker or Blue, but I knew that wouldn't happen. With the new cameras he'd installed, he could probably watch me do everything in this building, so he knew when and how to avoid me. It was so ridiculous. Three days ago the man was standing in the hallway with the biggest boner I'd ever seen, basically propositioning me, and I'd turned him down because I wanted more.

What an idiot I was.

I glanced down the hallway toward the manager's office, then away. He was probably there. Virginia said he hadn't left since I'd been having issues. I didn't need a phantom babysitter, though. With that thought in mind, I headed upstairs. Maybe I would pack up my laptop and get out of the building altogether. I needed groceries anyway.

Columbus had some of the most amazing coffee shops. Ohio State took up a significant part of the city and all of those sleep-deprived kids ran on caffeine. I picked a shop I hadn't been to often and drove there, settling in to suck up some Wi-Fi and stretch my mind.

I'd been there a few hours when I got a text message from Booker.

Where are you?

I told him.

Stay there.

What the hell... *Why?*

Because somebody just tried to kick down your door again. They didn't get through, but I got a notification of movement in your hall-way. Did your Ring pick anything up?

I backed out of the text page. Damn. There it was. I had a notification from six minutes ago. I pulled it up and looked at the image.

It was some guy in a clown face mask. He kicked at it several times, then seems to hurt himself. Lol. He walks away limping.

Send me that video. I think I found him on the other feeds as well.

I forwarded Booker the video. I was so glad we'd installed all that crap.

I tried to get back to work, but I was too busy looking at my phone and waiting for a message. Finally, I couldn't stand it any longer. I pressed the green phone button. Booker picked up almost immediately, like he'd been waiting for my call.

"We got a plate. Blue ran him down and we sat on him until the cops got here. He met somebody in the parking lot earlier this afternoon. I'm going to call my detective buddy and see what I can find out. You probably need to come home and file another report. They can look up the plate as well."

"Okay," I said, reaching for my laptop bag. "I'm on my way. I'm just a few minutes away."

Figures. I'd just ordered a fresh coffee. I carried the ceramic cup up to the clerk. "Can I get this in a to-go cup?"

The young woman smiled and nodded, taking it from me. I waited impatiently as she poured it into the cup and put the lid on it, then handed it over. I dropped another tip into her jar and headed out of the shop, laptop bag over my shoulder.

Almost immediately, I sensed the guy that fell into step behind me. He wasn't especially stealthy, so I didn't think he was out to harm me. Men had approached me before, thinking I needed attention. They could be so conceited.

I walked down the sidewalk and around the corner to the paid lot where I'd left my car. Trying to be subtle, I dug in my laptop bag for something and glanced behind my shoulder. The guy was gone. Relief flowed over me and I cursed my overactive sensitivity.

Waving at the attendant, I hustled toward my car, key fob in hand. Thinking about all the horror movies I'd seen in my life, I took a second to look beneath the car, then through the rear window of my SUV. Clear. I slipped inside, started the car and pulled out of the lot.

I'd barely gone a block when I felt a thumping in my wheel. I did not have a flat tire. I angled my mirrors down. Yep, there it was. Passenger side rear. Fuck!

There weren't a lot of places to pull over and work. Traffic was flowing and the parking spaces on the streets were full. Downtown Columbus in the middle of the day was hopping, and the drivers didn't give a fuck what your issues were, you needed to get out of their way. There was a church just ahead, maybe they had a lot I could get into.

I cranked the wheel and pulled into St. John's Church, then angled into the lot. I grabbed my phone and texted Booker that I had a flat and that I'd be there as soon as I could.

Climbing out of the car, I circled around to the rear hatch and popped it open. Papa had taught me to change my own tires. I'd never had to do this one though, because it was a new car.

It was a new car.

I circled around to look at the wheel, and the hairs crept up on my neck. That was a slice in the sidewall. It was one thing to drive around and pick up a nail or a screw. Columbus always seemed to be under construction, so it was expected. A cut in the sidewall was a very different thing. Someone had made that cut. I hadn't hit anything.

A truck pulled into the parking lot, and my fear shot through the roof. It was a big, overblown redneck truck, with an over-sized black pipe front bumper. A man in cowboy boots stepped out of the truck. He was about six feet tall and had a paunch. A ball cap sat low over his brow and I could see a frizzy, dark beard. Sunglasses shaded his eyes. There was nothing out of the ordinary about him, but the situation was out of the ordinary and I didn't trust his appearance. People could be considerate and stop for a woman on the side of the road, but I was in a parking lot off the road.

"I saw you pull in with a flat. Can I help you?"

"I would prefer not," I called out firmly.

The man walked toward me. "I'm not a stalker, or anything. I've got time to fix your flat if you let me get your tools out of the back."

"I said I'm fine. My fiancé is on his way."

The man looked around the lot and back out to the street. "He's not here now, though. I could have it done before he even got here."

He continued to walk toward me, and I prepared to jump in my car. Luckily, I'd left the driver's side door open. I slammed the back hatch with one hand and began backing away. That was when he lurched toward me.

This was not happening again! I jumped into my car and slammed and locked the doors. The man reached my window and tried to open the door. "You need to let me in if you want your tire changed."

"Fuck off!"

I started the car and hit the redial button on the audio system. Booker answered on the first ring. "There's a guy trying to break into my car. I'm in the St. John's parking lot with a flat and this guy stopped. He won't leave."

"I'm on my way," Booker said, and I could hear pounding footsteps as he took off. A dog barked in the background and it had to be Blue.

"Stay on the line, Cat," he puffed out.

"I am."

The man knocked on my window again. "At least pop your back hatch. I can work with you in there."

I snorted. There was no latch to pop. This was a Toyota and the biggest gripe I had about this vehicle was that the back gate was not electric. You had to lift it open and slam it shut. "I'm fine. You need to leave."

"I'm not leaving a woman alone in a parking lot," he called through the glass.

"It's a church. I'm fine. Leave!"

His lips curled and he reached for the door handle again. "Unlock it."

"Fuck you."

"Catalina," Booker growled, "put the car in drive and head toward me. Don't worry about the wheel. You need to get out of there. I'm coming up Spring and about to turn on South Third.

I'm three minutes out. Head toward 4th street and I'll come up behind you."

"Okay," I said, my heart pounding.

"Leave me on speaker phone so I can hear you," he yelled, and I mounted my phone on the windshield in its place.

I shifted into gear and pulled away from the man. My trusty car dragged a little with the flat, but I pressed down on the accelerator. In the rearview mirror I could see him run to his truck and hop in, then tires screeched as the truck surged behind me. My hands shaking, I gassed it to get to the street, but I reacted too slowly. The truck hit my car from behind, and the wheel jerked in my hands. I maintained control, but I glanced up in time to see the big iron bumper hit my vehicle again. The glass shattered in the back hatch and I screamed out as my car jolted over a parking spot block, then a second one. I kept the gas pedal down as the truck jolted after me.

"Motherfucker!" I yelled, bouncing in my seat.

I turned the wheel, trying to avoid running into a brick wall. It had been on the opposite side of the parking lot, but now it was looming close. There were no other cars in the lot other than a white church van, so I didn't worry about hitting anyone, but I didn't want to go to the street.

I glanced up and knew that the next strike was going to be devastating. The truck slammed into me and shoved my car across the lot. A split second later I hit the wall I'd been trying to avoid, and the truck slammed into my ass end, wedging me against the brick.

Knowing that if he got me pinned I was in trouble, I tried to get ready to scramble to the passenger side of the car. The man stepped out of his truck and marched toward my door. Scrambling, and for the first time so thankful I was small, I moved to the passenger side and pushed open the door. Something on it wasn't working right, so I really had to shove to get it open. Once I did, I took off running.

At that same moment a Columbus PD squad car sped into the lot, with Booker's truck right behind it. The PD car went for the truck, but Booker stopped right beside me and hopped out. Blue jumped out of the truck and raced after the guy that had hit me. He tackled him and bit his arm until the cops got there to take him. Booker called out a release and the dog trotted back to their side.

"Are you okay?"

I nodded, feeling like I had just run a marathon. My heart was trying to thud out of my chest, and everything was in super-sharp focus. Booker gripped my upper arms and leaned down to look in my eyes. "You're not hurt?"

"I don't think so," I said, trying to catch my breath. I turned, watching as the two officers rolled the guy over on the ground and piled on. Within seconds he was in cuffs and spouting curses at them, and me. When he saw me staring at them, his face purpled with rage. "You're going to regret this, bitch. You never should have put my brother in jail."

Well, hell. That answered a few questions. "So, if this is a brother I wonder if the other guy is a relative."

"More than likely."

This was ridiculous.

By the time we talked to the cops and explained the entire situation, the light was fading on the day, but Lincoln Holmes, Sean's brother, had been taken to jail. We had to wait for a detective to arrive, and I had to go through the same story again. Booker was also interviewed, and he provided them with copies of the pictures the cameras had caught. I also had to send the Ring video to Detective Spring.

The man looked at me incredulously as I explained every-thing that had happened in the past month. "Obviously he's going up for assault with a deadly weapon and probably intimidation of a witness. I'll subpoena his phone records. I have a suspicion they didn't bother covering their tracks. He doesn't seem especially sharp."

"Will Sean get more charges out of this as well? At least a protection order violation?" I asked.

"If I can connect the dots between the two brothers and the attacks, yes, he will. I'll talk to the DA tomorrow."

"And the other guy?"

"He'll be charged as well as soon as we identify him."

I looked up at Booker. He'd wrapped his big arm over my shoulders, holding me close to his side. Blue leaned into my thighs in comfort. A wrecker had already hauled Lincoln's truck away and another was idling across the lot, waiting for the go-ahead to hook up my poor Toyota. I'd called the insurance company and given them the police report number, and they promised to be in contact once they'd gotten the report. The vehicle was totaled, so I got everything out of it I could and stacked it in Booker's back seat. My laptop was still in its protective case and seemed to be okay as well.

Eventually, the scene wrapped up and Detective Spring told us we could go. I climbed into Booker's truck again and sagged into the seat. Blue jumped into the back seat. I stared out the window as the scenery passed by and wished I'd been able to salvage my coffee. Or maybe not. I looked down at my hands in my lap. They'd started to calm down. For a while they'd been shaking uncontrollably. I probably didn't need any more caffeine today.

Booker called Tanner on the way home. "Hey, Catalina. Glad you're okay. Boss, I checked the building and I don't see anything that needs fixed. All the cameras are working. It looks like he went straight to her door and when he couldn't get through, he left."

"Thanks, Tanner. I'll call you in the morning."

"Thanks, Tanner," I called to him. I looked up at Booker. "Thank you," I said simply. "I knew what I needed to do, but I appreciated you being on the line with me."

"Any time," he said quietly, his voice more raspy than usual. Then he reached over and gripped my hand.

Tears started in my eyes and I wanted to crawl across the seat and wrap myself around him, but I controlled myself.

I glanced around as he made a turn in the opposite direction from the Willows. I trusted him, so I didn't say anything, just held his hand and looked out the window. Eventually we pulled into a parking garage, with a heavy garage door rolling up to admit us, then rolling back down behind us. Booker pulled into a space and parked. Blue whined to be let out, and I finally let go of Booker's hand. I could tell he would have sat there all night if I'd needed him to.

Slipping out of the truck, I hiked my laptop bag onto my shoulder. My life was in this bag. Literally. Blue bounced around to me, wagging his little nubbin tail, and I stroked his beautiful dark head. "Where are we?" I asked, but I had an idea.

"This is my place. I sleep at the Willows, but this is home base."

I followed him onto the elevator, seeing all of the cameras strategically placed to have the best views of everything going on. "Do you own this one?"

He chuckled a little. "Maybe."

We landed at the top floor and he led me down a short hallway to the right, then used a broad-headed key to open a door. He waved me in. "Please make yourself comfortable."

Blue bounded in and immediately went to a box on the far side of the room that was full of dog toys. He chose one and started flinging his head around. It was obvious he was glad to be in his home space.

And it was a beautiful space. More of a studio, it had a huge expanse of open living area, broken up by a couple of clusters of furniture. There was a fireplace on the exterior wall, surrounded by glass windows and high ceilings. It was a beautiful space, and it looked like he'd had a designer come in to decorate it.

I gravitated toward one corner of the studio. There was a green velvet pool table set and ready for the break. Several arcade games lined the wall, and my hands drifted over them. "I remember this one," I breathed, smiling at him over my shoulder. "They used to have them in Pizza Shacks and you could play them while you waited for your pizza to be ready."

"Yes. Some of my favorite memories."

I nodded. "Mine too."

Moving on around the room, I found more personality than I had with his other apartment. Not that I'd been in there much. There was a pretty oak bar in this corner, but it didn't look well-used. It just looked like a display.

"It's handy if I have people over who drink."

"True," I said, moving along. I came to a long, heavy book-case full of books and memorabilia. Booker liked to read crime thrillers. And biographies. Then there was a shelf of pictures, and I got choked up. This must be his Ranger team. In every picture, he wore fatigues and carried a lethal-looking weapon. He stood with other men dressed the same way, and there was a comfort level that was almost visible. These men had been through a lot together, and it was obvious they knew each other well. In two pictures, Booker was even grinning, looking hand-some and relaxed despite the unfamiliar terrain behind them, wearing a tan beret. They had to be overseas.

"I don't know anything about Army Rangers other than that they're badasses," I admitted.

"I'm not a Ranger anymore," he said softly.

Giving him a face, I glanced at him. "Right."

It seemed like he was always next to one particular ginger-haired man. "Who's this?"

"His name was Thomas Paronto. We went through Ranger school and were assigned to the 2nd Battalion, 75th Ranger Regiment. He was my best friend."

"Was?" I hated to ask because I thought I knew.

"Yes. He died three days after we were hit. We were shipped stateside together, and that was the last time I saw him."

"I'm sorry, Booker."

He blinked and turned to walk into the kitchen. "Not your fault."

The way he said it made me think he considered it completely *his* fault. I followed along behind him. "It's not your fault either," I said.

Pulling a glass from the cupboard, he ran it full of water from the fridge and handed it to me, then got a second one for himself. He drank most of it down before he looked at me. "I know that, theoretically. There's this what-if game, though, that I play in my head over and over again."

Snorting, I set the glass down. "We all do that. I mean, what if I'd told Sean no when he'd first asked me out? Yeah, he wouldn't have taken me out, but I wouldn't have had a chance to get to know you either. Out of this entire fiasco, I consider meeting you and getting to know you the silver lining to it all."

Booker shook his head and ran a hand through his hair. He seemed agitated, and I didn't know if it was because I was in his personal space or because we were talking about his guilt. Probably a combination of the two.

"It's hard to know what would have happened if you had stayed," I told him. "You both might have died."

"That may not have been a bad thing," he said, avoiding my eyes.

Anger spiked in my gut and I reached for his arm, turning

him to face me. "You don't say stuff like that. It would not have been better if you'd died. If you had, I would have been dead. Or hoping I died because I was recovering from being raped and beaten in my own apartment. Would that have been better?"

"Of course not," he said, finally looking at me.

"Things happen for a reason, and I think you were meant to be here with me. I know I'm so thankful you are." Stepping forward, I wrapped my arms around his waist and rested my head on his chest. It took him a minute to wrap his arms around me, and I worried he wouldn't. Eventually, he did, and he rested his cheek against my head. He heaved a heavy breath and seemed to relax into my hold.

11

C at stepped into my arms and everything swung around. The anxiety I'd been feeling about protecting her had eased because she was in the building and behind locked doors, but a new one had taken its place. Now she was in my space, and I had to explain pieces of my life to her I didn't want to revisit at all. The little bit I'd told her, though, didn't seem to hurt as bad with her.

And now that I was holding her, I had a new fear. It was very easy to hold her and let my concerns drift away. If she left like I expected her to, my emotions were going to be shredded. Again.

"Thank you for being you, Gabriel Booker."

It was a shock hearing my own name. I used Gabriel so little. The sound of my name on her lips was very sexy, though, and I really didn't mind it. Her hands were rubbing up and down my back, making my emotions head in a completely different direction.

Cat must have felt me responding, because she leaned back to give me a serious look. Then, before I could offer to let her go, she went up on tiptoe and kissed me. Oh, damn... the woman had the most extraordinary mouth and I had to respond.

Cupping her head in my hands, I angled my mouth over hers, my tongue sweeping into her sweetness. I went from semi-interested to hard as a rock within seconds, and she gasped in a breath. "Gabriel," she breathed, and something clutched in my chest.

The woman was going to kill me with her sweetness.

Cat's hands, half the size of my own, reached down to cup my ass and I knew something was going to happen soon. Cat must have thought the same because she reached for the button on my jeans, popping it free, then lowering my zipper. Within seconds her hand was inside the fabric and I was even closer to losing my sanity.

Reaching for the hem of her shirt, I pulled it over her head. She reached behind herself and unfastened her bra, flinging it aside. Then I was looking down at her cleavage pressed against my chest. I scraped her nipples with my thumbnails and lifted the weight. They were so beautiful in my hands. I pressed them together, feeling the softness, and I wanted to taste them.

I reached for her hips to lift her onto the counter, but she stopped me. Bending over she ripped off her jeans and panties, standing naked before me. It should have been scandalous, looking at her in the kitchen like this, but I'd bought this building for its security and privacy. No one would see us.

Knowing that the granite counter would be cold, I ripped off my T-shirt and straightened it across the surface. Then I lifted her to the edge. With one hand, I checked her readiness. She was drenched, and I couldn't help but play as I grew even harder.

"I need you to love me, Gabriel," she panted, lifting her mouth to mine.

As much as I wanted to slam into her and ride her hard, I knew she needed more time. Just a few more seconds, then I would take her. I lifted her to the edge of the counter, and spread her knees.

I worked my thumb through her pretty folds and inserted my middle finger deep into her body. She cried out, her head falling back on her neck. She clutched my shoulders in her hands and braced her feet wide to give me easier access. I swirled my thumb around, finding her clit. Then I worked my thumb and middle finger together in a hard rhythm. Groaning, she rocked her hips up and I felt the subtle pulse of her body around my hand. I kept moving, knowing she would reach her orgasm soon.

With a panting cry, she arched back on the island. I exchanged my hand for my mouth, teasing her into another wave of climax with my tongue. She tasted so sweet. Shivers danced over her body and she clutched my head in her hands, riding my mouth until her orgasm faded away.

Even then, she pulled me to her, and into her, silky smooth heat wrapping around my dick. I was already at the edge of my control and she didn't help with that move. Her body was the perfect height for me to grind into her, then pull out. I looked down at where we were joined, and almost came just from the visual. I drew out, then pushed deep, making her cry out. I built a rhythm, holding her hips as I withdrew, then surged back in. Every time I slammed into her, her breasts bounced, and it was so fucking hot.

My balls tightened and I knew I was done. The orgasm stole my rhythm and arched me back, seated as deep as I could be in her. My leg went weak and I almost went down, but she grabbed me around the back and gave me some support. It was perfect.

When I was able to regain my feet and my breath, I looked down at her. She gave me this beautiful, serene smile, and leaned up to kiss my chin. "I really like your kitchen."

I barked out a laugh and clutched her hips in my hands.

Concentrating very carefully, I wrapped her legs around my hips and carried her into the bedroom, then on through to the bathroom. Years ago, when I'd first had the amputation, they'd told me that I would never be able to carry more than twenty-five pounds at a time, because my leg would give out.

I was glad I could prove them wrong, I thought, grinning.

"You seem very satisfied with yourself," Cat murmured, her arms around my neck.

"I am," I told her, and repeated what the doctor had said so long ago.

"Fuck him," she said, scoffing. "Obviously he must not have dealt with many Army Rangers."

I laughed again, even as I set her down beside the glass walled shower. The complete confidence in my abilities was a little humbling, but then, she'd never voiced a hint of doubt that I could do anything. The disability was not a disability to her. I felt lighter in my skin, knowing that she had that confidence in me.

"I need to change out my leg," I told her.

"Ah, I wondered how you did that."

Reaching around her for the taps, I turned the shower on and set the temp. There was a steam option I thought she might like, so I turned it on as well.

"Oh, wow," she breathed. She ripped off her socks, the only things left on, and stepped into the steam. I watched her for a moment, literally entranced as the steam seemed to wrap around her voluptuous curves.

My shower leg stood against the wall of the shower, near a bench. I stripped off my hanging jeans and underwear, then sat down to remove my prosthetic leg. I broke the seal on the cup and rolled the sock down, exposing the stump. Then I pulled the shower leg in and reset the stump. The shower leg didn't fit as well as my fitted prosthetic, but it had a lot better grip for the tile.

Catalina watched me as I stepped into the steam, a gentle smile on her full mouth. "How long ago did you lose your leg?"

"Seven years ago. It started as just my foot, then I got an infection and they had to do a below-knee amputation."

She rested her hands on my chest as she looked up at me. "That must have been incredibly hard."

"It was," I agreed, "but I think my parents took it worse. I'd been their perfect football player son, and then I was just broken. I had shrapnel wounds all over my body. One of the pieces went through my vocal cords. It's why my voice is so raspy."

"I love your voice. It seems to suit your look," she grinned, running her hand down my goatee. I needed to trim it up, but I hadn't had a chance to in the last few days. Too much other stuff going on.

"So, do you think it's done," she asked, shifting gears.

I sighed as I looked down at her. "I have no idea, honestly. He could have been done with everything, but he's stacking charges on top of charges, and dragging the Holoman family into it."

"I think he had two brothers and I remember him talking about getting together with his cousins a lot. His dad is the one that runs the family business, though. I remember we were supposed to go to dinner with them and it fell through for some reason."

"What's the family business?"

She scrunched up her nose. "It's something to do with construction. Heavy equipment."

Hm. There was a chance I knew them then. Great...

Cat poured a dollop of my shower gel into her hand and started lathering her hair and body, and I lost all awareness. I just stood there watching her hands glide over her round hips and up her breasts. This image was going to haunt me for the rest of my life.

She rinsed off, squirted another dollop of gel into her hand, and started lathering me. "I love the way you smell," she said over the sound of the water.

Cat worked over my chest, down my belly and to my groin, then she swept around my flanks. "Turn around," she told me, and I did. Then she scrubbed my back with a shower poof I had never used before, and I wanted to sag against the wall. That was bone-melting. My back itched in places I'd never noticed before, but she took care of them all. Then she shifted back around to the front and started working down my legs. When she prodded my right leg, I reluctantly lifted it out of the cup of the shower leg. She ran her hands over the stump so matter-of-factly, I couldn't believe it. Then she moved to the other leg.

She lathered every inch of my skin, then used the hand shower to rinse me down. I took a minute to wash my hair, then rinsed again. My emotions were kind of in a spin, so I finished mechanically, and stepped out of the shower.

"Did I do something wrong?" Cat asked, stepping out behind me.

"No, not at all."

I dried off and headed toward the bedroom, grabbing my regular prosthetic on the way, then I headed for the closet to grab a fresh amputation sock.

"Um, do you think I can borrow a t-shirt and a pair of shorts or something?"

Oh, yeah, she had her dirty clothes and that was it. "Sure," I said, snatching a tee off the hanger and digging for a pair of shorts. I handed them to her and watched as she dressed, unself-conscious. I thought I'd gotten over being self-conscious, but she stirred all those feelings up again. I wanted to be more for her.

My leg wasn't magically going to reappear, though. That was a dead end. And TBIs generally didn't just get better. They became idiosyncrasies that had to be dealt with every day. So far I hadn't had any of my really bad outbursts, and I hadn't had any mood swings since the day Sean had struck me in the skull. I'd had a few lapses in concentration, but those were pretty easily dealt with. Last week had been the worst issue. I'd climbed into my truck and just sat there, not sure what to do. I'd looked around, and I had the keys in my hand, but I couldn't connect the dots on what to do. It had taken me almost half an hour to turn the key and remember how to drive.

I'm glad things like that didn't happen very often, because I would never want to be a danger to the public.

I found that when I was concentrating on a task, those issues didn't bother me as much. So, long-running tasks that kept my mind engaged kept my brain busy. Every once in a while there was a short in the system, but I rolled with it and kept going.

"I think you'll have to run me home," Cat said, sitting on the edge of my bed.

"What was that?"

"You'll have to run me home."

The t-shirt was big overall, but her breasts managed to fill it out. She had one knee folded up on the mattress, and her pale legs drew my attention. They were short and delicately shaped and beautiful. I wanted to kiss all the way up their length, to the honey at her core. Her toenails were a bright aqua, and I couldn't help but grin at the cheery color. It suited her personality so well.

"This is a safe place. Why don't you stay here for a while?"

Her brows lifted as she looked at me. "Um, I don't know, Booker. As lovely as your place is, I'm not sure that I should stay here, for a couple of reasons. Number one, you seem a little protective of your space."

I winced, because she was right. I never brought women here. This was a true bachelor pad, and hardly anyone even knew I lived here.

"That's fine," she continued. "You've stated that you don't want to take our friendship further and I respect that. And I understand you have some hang ups about your body."

My mouth opened and I blinked. "Well, wouldn't you?"

I held the stump up for emphasis.

She shook her head and heaved a sigh. "I know you think that's a turnoff for me, but it really isn't. Do you think I haven't struggled with my own body issues? I mean, there's no straightening these curves." She stood up and patted her gently rounded ass. "And I've come to accept that. The loss of your leg is tragic, but it doesn't make you any less appealing to me. And your voice... sends shivers down my spine," she said, walking toward me. "And the hearing loss on this side," she motioned to my left ear, "doesn't bother me. I just shift to the right."

I cringed, because I hadn't told her about that. And if I hadn't told her about it, she had noticed on her own. How many other people had noticed?

"These are all signs of a warrior." Her fingers danced over the slight scars I knew marked my neck. "And a hero."

I shook my head, thinking about all of the things I hadn't done right. I wasn't a hero. If I was, I'd have realized she was still having issues even after Sean had been arrested. If I was a hero, I'd have seen the ambush we were rolling into, or I would have stopped Paronto's bleeding faster. There were so many things that made me *not* a hero.

"And right here," she said, running her hand over my tense face. "I can see you arguing with yourself. Denying yourself happiness when you don't have to. I know you carry a lot of needless guilt. It's all part of your honor. I get that. But you're denying yourself happiness, Gabriel Booker. You're denying yourself love."

Cat leaned up and pressed a kiss to my lips. It was a soft, lingering kiss, and I wanted to hold her to me. It would be better for her, though, if I let her go.

"I'll get dressed and drive you," I said, my voice no louder than a whisper.

I thought she would cry, but this incredibly sad expression settled on her face, and I wondered if I was doing the right thing. I'd never dared dream we could actually be together long-term. I planned on enjoying being with her in the moment, and after her history I thought she'd not want anything long-term.

I HELD it together all the way home. Booker circled the building and parked in the manager's spot. Blue jumped down out of the truck and raced around the back, looking for stray cats. There was a small patch of grass with a sign in the middle. He circled the post and peed a little, then raced to the back door.

Booker had his key out and was getting ready to unlock the door, when a young man approached us from the side. Had he been leaning against the wall? He asked us to hold on. "Are you Catalina Rivera?"

Booker immediately stepped in front of me, his broad back keeping me from seeing the young man.

"Who's asking?"

"My name is Alexander Holoman, and my grandfather Jeffrey would like to extend an invitation to Ms. Rivera for a cup of coffee. There have been some... incidents, and he would appreciate a chance to talk to Ms. Rivera. In a public place, of course. He understands that she has no reason to trust, but hopes that she will give him the benefit of the doubt."

I peered around Booker's shoulder. The kid appeared to be as young as he sounded, maybe just early twenties. Booker's arms were crossed over his chest, and he was glaring at the kid. I looked at him and his mouth twisted as he shrugged. It was up to me.

I sighed, wondering if Sean's Dad had more control over him than anyone else. I looked at the young messenger. He seemed earnest and sincere, and I wondered who his father was. "Is Sean your uncle?"

"Yes," he replied, and he said the word carefully, as if to keep hidden emotion out of it. Or to reluctantly acknowledge the fact.

"Then your father is..."

"Chad Holoman."

The name rang a bell, like Sean had been bitching about him, maybe. Or something. "It's too late tonight. Can I meet him tomorrow?"

Alexander smiled. "That's what he expected. 10 a.m. at Uncommon Grounds?"

That was the closest coffee shop to my building. "That's fine. I'll see him tomorrow."

Alexander gave a wave. "Thank you, ma'am."

He jogged toward the street and got into a sporty little car. Looked expensive.

"I don't know if this is a good idea," Booker murmured.

"Well, considering two of his sons have tried to beat the crap out of me, this was a nice invitation. I'm curious to see what he says."

Sighing like I was trying his last nerve, Booker unlocked the door and walked me to the elevator, then he held the door while I got on. A draft ran into the car, chilling my bare legs. I'd shoved my dirty clothes into my computer bag, and it was so weird running around without panties on. I felt more vulnerable and unsupported.

"I don't know how men go commando," I murmured. "It would drive me nuts. No pun."

Booker chuckled. "Not something I understand either."

We walked down the hallway to my door, Blue running ahead to sniff. He must have been caught by the Ring because I felt the notification hit my phone.

Anxiety churned in my stomach, and I wondered what the hell to do. Should I invite Booker in? That might lead to more sex, and while that was supremely enjoyable, I wasn't sure it was good for whatever relationship we had.

Actually, I was beginning to feel sore. Another scalding hot shower and bed sounded nice.

"Why don't you go take a few ibuprofen. You'll probably be sore tomorrow. I'll be here at nine-thirty to pick you up."

I pulled out my keys and unlocked my door, already shaking my head. "I appreciate that, but no need. I'm going to do it alone. And I will get some ibuprofen. Thank you, Booker. You've really been..." I looked down at my hands, my throat aching with emotion. "You've really been a warrior for me."

I wanted to say so much more, but he wasn't ready for it.

"Don't thank me. Just be safe," he said, his voice raspy. "Blue!" he snapped. With a final, dark look, Blue turned and walked down the hallway after Booker. Then he hesitated, glancing back like he wanted to stay.

"Go on, buddy," I said, motioning with my hand.

I made sure I was inside, away from the cameras, before I let the tears fall.

～

I WOKE with the headache from hell. That's what I got when I slept on the couch feeling sorry for myself. My mouth tasted like shit, too, because I hadn't been motivated enough to get up and brush my teeth before bed. I glanced at the clock on the kitchen wall. I had two hours before I needed to be at the coffee shop.

Just enough time to take yet another shower because my boobs were sticky from the ice cream I'd dripped on my chest last night. Guess there were worse things to get obliterated on than Moose Tracks.

I was at a loss as to what to do about Booker. The man was a dream. Literally and figuratively. I didn't understand why he was so determined to be alone. Rolling off the couch, I padded to the kitchen for a cup of cream with a splash of coffee. I carried it to the office and tried to wake up as I scanned news article after news article about veterans, specifically those with TBI. There were several things that kept popping up and making me think of Booker.

One was survivor's guilt. It was obvious that he struggled with it. I knew he had a TBI when he was deployed, and that survivor guilt could be exacerbated by the TBI.

It could also cause unnatural anxiety, or spikes in anxiety. I hadn't asked him what kind of medication he was on, if any, but there were treatments available.

I got lost in the research, just like I always did, and I had to scramble to get myself cleaned up in time for my coffee date. Or appointment. Judgement. Threat. Whatever it was. There was a very real chance that I would go to this appointment and have to file another police report. I actually debated calling the police just to make sure I wasn't being an idiot in doing this.

The thought gave me anxiety. Maybe *I* needed medication for my life.

I dressed and did my hair, put on some makeup. Debated whether or not to take my computer. Decided against it, in case I needed to run or fight.

What the hell was my life coming to?

I called for an Uber, not an app I'd used recently since I'd moved away from the center of town. But until insurance replaced my car, I was a pedestrian.

The Uber driver matched her profile and seemed really nice, and she didn't talk very much. I wasn't sure I could respond anyway, because my gut was in knots. Maybe I should have had Booker come with me. Then I would have had backup.

Ugh. I hated this. I just wanted my life to go back to normal. But that wasn't even right. I wanted my life to be normal, plus Gabriel Booker. And Blue. They came as a package.

The coffee shop was moderately crowded, which made me feel better about meeting here. Would they try something with this many witnesses? I scanned the crowd, but didn't see Alexander, so I headed to the counter for my coffee. I doubted I would be able to drink, but we'd see.

The barista was sweet and chatted as she made my drink, but I was watching the front door for people entering. So, I saw the older man when he entered. He looked like an older version of Sean, a little heavier set with bright blue eyes. He spotted me when he came in and gave me a wave, then headed toward an unoccupied table on the far side of the room. I was surprised he didn't order a coffee, but maybe this wasn't his kind of place.

Taking my drink, I headed over to the table, sitting down across from the man. He held his hand out as soon as I was settled. "My name is Jeffrey Holoman, and I thank you for coming to meet me, Ms. Rivera. I don't suppose you have a great appreciation for my family right now."

"I have to say, I'm guarded," I admitted, but I shook his hand.

His blue eyes narrowed a little as he gave me a gentle smile. "Understandable. I've read the police reports and the witness statements. Can you give me an idea of what happened to start it all? Why are two of my boys in jail?"

I blinked. "It doesn't matter how it started. Our relationship was not doing well to begin with."

"Ah, okay." Jeffrey sat back in his chair. "He had talked about bringing you to a family dinner because you were a good girl. He thought I would like you."

I smiled, but I had a feeling it looked strained. There was no sense going over all this. "Perhaps."

"Well, I suppose I don't blame you for being circumspect. What it boils down to is, you are not to blame for the actions of my boys, and I'm here to apologize on behalf of the family." He frowned, age lines bracketing his mouth, and I realized he had to be nearing retirement. Did 'the boys' work with him in the family business?

"It's not your fault," I told him, and the words were completely true. Sean was in his late thirties and well able to decide his own path in life, and Lincoln had to be older than that. "Has he done this with a woman before? Or Lincoln? Maybe you need to have a talk with them about priorities and behavior and family honor."

I slammed my mouth shut, but it was said, and I waited for the fallout.

Jeffrey smiled, but it was incredibly sad. "I have, until I'm blue in the face. If it wasn't for my other son and my grandson, I would think the Holoman name was destined to die out known as criminals and thugs."

It was weird, but I felt like he was looking for some kind of reassurance. "I can tell Alexander has been brought up right."

A wide smile spread across his face. "I love that boy. He does everything we ask and more. Honestly, I would trust him to run the business before Sean. I just don't know where I went wrong with that boy."

I shook my head, not willing to comment on that one. "Please, let him deal with the repercussions. Don't bail him or

Lincoln out. If they continue on their path, they're going to kill someone, or seriously maim someone. I was in genuine fear for my life yesterday, and Lincoln was not stopping until he totaled my car."

Jeffrey frowned and I knew it had to be hard hearing he needed to let his own sons suffer. They wouldn't learn, otherwise. He sighed, looking down at his clasped hands. "Lincoln has always looked up to Sean, no matter what, and he's followed him down every path, right or wrong. And I'll admit, I've helped my boys out before, but this time they went too far."

"You think? Sean literally kicked my door in. Do you know how terrifying that is for a woman alone? If Booker hadn't been there, I'd be in the hospital or dead. I have no doubt of that in my mind. Sean put him in the hospital. He had to get stitches in his stomach, and he could have lost the use of his hand, because Sean brought a weapon to see me."

Jeffrey's eyes hardened, and he nodded. "I've read the report, and I can't believe they went so far..." he stuttered to a halt, and I gave him a sharp look.

"This time?" I demanded. "Is that what you were going to say? This time?"

He heaved another sigh and gave me a narrow-eyed look. He didn't like being put on the spot. "There was an incident a few years ago. Similar situation. The girl chose to drop the charges."

"When you offered her money?" I asked, rocking back in my chair.

"There was a settlement involved," he conceded.

"I'm not dropping the charges." Anger was boiling in my gut.

He held up a hand. "I'm not asking you to. I'm trying to apologize." He looked out the window for a minute. "I'm telling you that I screwed up when I didn't believe the first girl, and I'm sorry you had to pay for my inaction."

Oh. That kind of depleted my anger. I could tell just by

looking in his eyes that he was sincere. "Thank you for that," I said softly. "I'm sorry for thinking the worst of you. I came to this meeting expecting to have to call the cops again."

Jeffrey shook his head. "No need for the police. I just wanted to let you know that I was sorry, and that I would not be helping my boys this time. They dug themselves this hole, and I'm not getting them out of it."

"I don't know that you could," I told him honestly. "Sean hit a cop. Lincoln damaged church property and totaled my car. Aggravated assault. I think they're beyond what you can help."

His jaw tightened and he looked down at his hands. "I know." He gave me a sad smile. "Not to make excuses, but they lost their mother a few years ago. Since then they've been acting out."

I looked him askance. "Jeffrey, I'm sorry you lost your wife, but you're talking about two men in their thirties, not teenagers, committing criminal acts. And you keep calling them 'the boys.' They're grown men. They should have their shit together by now."

For a moment Jeffrey stared at me, then he blinked. "Yes, you're completely right. I'm sorry." He pushed up from the chair. "On behalf of myself and the Holoman family, I apologize for my sons, Ms. Rivera. I will not pay for or support their legal defense, and if I speak to them, I will encourage them to plead guilty and do whatever time they're given. They have behaved abominably and I will not have it in my family." He pulled out a business card and set it on the table in front of me. "If for any reason you need anything, this is my personal number."

The man left soon after that, and I wasn't sorry to see him go. I sat there for a good while, though, just digesting. I hope he let them deal with their own consequences this time. After a lifetime of bailing them out, I wasn't sure he could change.

12

I watched the older man drive away. There was devastation on his face. Whatever Cat had said to the man had apparently reverberated.

She continued to sit at the table, playing with her coffee cup, but she wasn't crying or especially emotional. I picked up my phone from the console.

How did it go?

I watched her reach for her phone. *Lol! Fine. Too much to type. Why don't you come in?*

Well, hell. I sighed as I glanced up at her. She was looking right at me.

"Hey," I said when I walked in and took the seat the older man had been sitting in. "I was a Ranger, not a ninja."

It was worth the self-deprecation just to see her laugh. I grinned and shrugged. "So, what did he say?"

"That his boys had had it rough since their mother died. He apologized for them, like they were children. Promised that he wouldn't bail them out like the last time he did."

"No way," I breathed. My anger fired. I should have beat

Sean's ass more. There was no sense in a grown-ass man, two of them, behaving that way.

She recapped the entire conversation, and I stared at her. "I can't believe you pinned him like that. You've got balls, woman."

"Well, we'll see if he sticks to it. I can only imagine how protective I would be if it were my kids."

"You would never raise self-centered pricks like he did," I hiked my thumb over my shoulder, in the direction Jeffrey had gone.

Her cheeks took on a pink hue. "No, I wouldn't. I don't think you would either."

I shrugged. Kids weren't on my list of projects in the near future.

"I feel pretty good about him. Jeffrey, I mean. He has to lead by example for his other son and grandson."

"True," I said, watching her carefully. "You're sure he wasn't trying to pay you off?"

Cat shook her head. "I'm almost positive he wasn't. There was a feeling of resolve, like everything had come down on him at once. He was struggling, but I think he'll stick to his word because he has the rest of his family to look out for."

"I guess we'll have to wait and see."

Cat cocked her head at me. "You're trying to be a hero, again."

I shook my head. "You're the hero for standing up and dealing with these guys. I'm just backup."

She reached across and gripped my hand, palm to palm. "Still, I appreciate it. I didn't know what I was walking into."

Her hand pulled back a little, and her fingers traced along my palm, then down my fingers. I left my hand on the table, just soaking up her touch. I worried that every time I saw her might be the last, so I needed to remember every moment.

She turned my hand over, tracing the scar on the palm. "You've done so much for me, and I love you for it. You're an incredible man, Gabriel Booker."

It took me a minute to realize she'd just told me she loved me. I know my mouth fell open before I snapped it shut. Cat smiled gently and gathered up her bag, then she circled the table. With a hand under my chin, she kissed me, and it felt like a goodbye kiss.

"If you trust me to do this, you should trust that I know that I love you. And that you're worth loving. If you ever get to that point, let me know."

"I'll drive you home," I said, scrambling, but she pressed down on my shoulder.

"I'm fine. I have an Uber here to take me. Give Blue a hug for me."

And she walked out.

Though she'd been kind, I felt like I'd just been sucker-punched. How could I blame her, though? She deserved more than just the pieces I was willing to give her.

I'd trusted before, though, and it had almost killed me when I lost him. Besides that, I didn't think she had any idea what she would be dealing with down the road. The closer she got, the more chance there would be that I could hurt her.

I sat there for about an hour just staring into nothing, wondering what I should do, before I decided to head home. Maybe if I took one thing at a time, I would be able to move on.

Anger suddenly overwhelmed me, and my hands quaked with it. I looked around the coffee shop at all the normal people and wanted to scream at them. But I didn't know what I wanted to scream. I just wanted to voice my frustration and pain, and throw tables and chairs or something. I wanted to lash out like a child.

I knew what I was feeling was exacerbated by the TBI, though. And that knowledge was enough to let me start to calm down. I sat in that chair, with my hands clenched around the edges in a death grip, breathing repetitively, like I'd been trained. A few people gave me odd looks, but everyone left me alone, which was good. It enabled me to get a hold of myself.

By the time I climbed back into the truck, two hours had passed. It had been a blink of time in my mind, but there was no denying the numbers on the dash. It had been a little more than two hours. What the hell.

I went to the manager's apartment, but I didn't want to see anyone, so I packed up the few belongings I had moved over here and walked them to the truck. Blue danced around anxiously, not understanding the anger I had to be radiating. At one point he wedged himself against my legs when I stopped, and I looked down at him. There was concern, there. He knew his pack leader wasn't happy, and he would do whatever he needed to in order to get me in the right mood.

"I'm sorry, buddy," I murmured, leaning against the wall and rubbing the base of his ears. That's where he really liked it. And just the act of comforting my dog comforted me.

Once I'd calmed down, I locked up the manager's office apartment and headed down the hallway. I would have Tanner step in for a while, until I found someone permanent. Tomorrow I would list the job on the hiring sites.

Blue followed along as we headed to the truck for the final time. He loaded into the back seat and wagged his butt, just happy to be going anywhere.

I wish I could be a dog...

∽

I DIDN'T SEE or hear from Booker, and it made my heart ache.

Virginia said that Tanner had been taking care of the maintenance stuff, and that Booker had left the building. Completely. Ads had been placed to find a new building manager, and the job came with the attached apartment.

Which meant he'd moved out.

I left Virginia's, went upstairs and cried. I didn't understand how I kept screwing up with men. Was I a drama magnet? Was the drama why he didn't want to deal with me? Sean had pled not guilty to all charges, so it was going to go to trial, unless he eventually took a plea deal. So, I would be dealing with him for the foreseeable future. That was a lot to expect a guy to deal with, even if they were in love.

Booker was a gorgeous man with a true, honorable heart, but he was an unreachable dream.

I threw myself into work, signing up for a tech job site to make myself even busier. If I had projects, maybe it would keep me focused. The creativity was struggling, though. Every idea I had was like pulling teeth, and nothing ever satisfied. I wanted to take some time off, but I didn't want to backslide with my connections. I had worked hard to get where I was.

So, I put my head down and kept working. And tried to stop mourning Booker.

Then, almost two weeks after he moved out, I got an email.

Holy shit. The Love Vixen would be reading my email on tonight's show.

My normal, level-headed self kind of lost her marbles. I had already planned to go to Virginia's tonight for the listen party, but if I remembered correctly, I had offered to make him dinner and dessert.

Would he even hear the podcast? Should I have Virginia send him a message or something? Or maybe Tanner? Just to make sure he listened?

What should I make for dinner?

I needed to read the damned email and make sure that's what I'd said...

I needed to shave my legs...

I glanced at the clock. I had four hours to get myself together. And even that probably wasn't going to be long enough.

I couldn't go to Virginia's tonight. Not if I invited him to dinner here.

Needing a second opinion, I slipped on my shoes and headed out the door and down to Virginia's.

A smile cracked her face when she opened the door. "You're early, Catalina."

"I know, but I need to talk to you. I emailed the Love Vixen, and she's reading my email on the air tonight!"

I slapped a hand over my mouth, because my voice had progressively gotten louder.

Virginia's eyes got wide and she clapped her hands together. "Oh, honey! That's amazing news. What did you say in the email?"

I recapped what I'd said, and her eyes grew moist. "I'm sorry you've had so many problems recently, Catalina. I knew part of it, but I didn't realize you'd fallen in love with the man. That is really something special."

She looked out the window for a minute. "You need to go cook the man dinner, of course. Don't worry about my party. Go cook him something sexy, like pasta. And put your girls on display," she grinned.

I laughed. "Not like they aren't on display all the time," I murmured.

"Well, take some extra time tonight." Virginia leaned up and pressed a kiss to my cheek. "I expect details tomorrow, young woman! Oh, my gosh, you're going to be so popular in the building," she giggled.

So, I did as Virginia suggested. I went upstairs and started defrosting some chicken breasts. I could make a mean grilled chicken Alfredo. I had garlic cheese bread in the freezer. And bagged salad in the crisper. Ok, that was ready. I had a bunch of apples, so I started slicing them up for a cobbler. That would be good and easy.

Then I went and showered, taking extra time with my hair. I shaved every inch of my legs and my arm pits, hoping I didn't miss anything unsightly. I plucked my brows and lotioned up from top to bottom. Then I took almost thirty minutes to dry my mass of hair, styling it into big, uniform curls. I very carefully applied make-up, then a finishing spray to keep it on. Okay, I looked pretty damned good. This was the most dressed up I'd gotten for a long time, and I didn't think Booker had ever seen me this way.

So, I hope it worked.

Now, what do I wear? How should I look? Casual and easy? Or dress up and expect roses? I wrinkled my nose as I went through the closet. Nice fitting jeans and a pretty shirt, I decided, with little ankle boots. It was put together but not too over the top.

A half hour before the eight p.m. broadcast, I started cooking chicken breast. If he was across town in his apartment, it would take him a half hour to get to me.

And this was all assuming that he even responded. I was pinning my hopes on a damn podcast he may or may not listen to.

At eight p.m., I turned on the podcast. The Alfredo simmered on the stove, waiting to be eaten, but I had to get it done early. I knew there was no way I could listen and cook at the same time. The apple crumble was in the oven and the timer was set.

I listened to the intro, butterflies dancing in my belly. I sat on the couch and folded my feet beneath me, anxiety churning.

Booker knew that I loved him, but now I was announcing it to everyone.

Fuck. This was an incredibly bad idea.

The Love Vixen had a lovely voice, and a lilting cadence. Even as she doled out common-sense advice, there was a hint of gentle teasing in her voice.

"This next email is from Desperate in Columbus."

My heart stalled in my chest.

Dear Vixen,

Please help me!

My hunky and reclusive next door neighbor is a true hero. When my ex busted down my door and attacked me, my neighbor Booker saved me, at extreme cost to himself. He knocked the guy out and watched over me until the police could haul my assailant away. Then he let me patch him up, but the caring led to more. We spent one beautiful night together, but he hasn't spoken to me very much since. Actually, he's gone to extreme lengths to avoid me, telling me what we had wasn't going anywhere.

Now, though, things are happening that make me think my ex is stalking me, and Booker is here to watch out for me. I'm afraid it won't last long, because there's a part of him that just won't let me in. I've tried to connect with him but he's a wounded veteran, a U.S. Army Ranger, and I believe he thinks everything I do is because I pity him or something. I just want to get to know him. I have no regrets from loving him and I hope he doesn't either. I can tell he's an incredible, honorable man, something we women dream of finding, but rarely do.

I'm afraid I've fallen for an unreachable dream.

I'm hoping that you will read this on your podcast on Friday. I've caught my neighbor listening to your show a couple of times, and I think it may be the only way I can get my message across to him.

Booker, if you're listening, come knock on my door. Dinner is ready. Dessert is optional.

I held my breath as I waited her response.

Dear Desperate,

First let me say, our nation's veterans have had a rough road, and they don't get the thanks and appreciation that they deserve.

Sweetie, congrats for rising above an unhealthy relationship with a hopeful heart. That took courage and determination. Something you and your neighbor have in common.

If your neighbor is fighting his attraction to you, I have to wonder what has caused him to be distrustful and to close his heart. I think finding that reason may be the key to happiness.

Take your time and be persistent. All good things come to those who are patient and he sounds like a gem worth waiting for!

Booker, if you're listening, take the chance and follow your heart. Go eat dessert.

Good luck, hon!

I sank back into the cushions of the couch, strangely giddy and calm, absorbing her words of advice. Yes, I did have a hopeful heart, in spite of my less-than-stellar track record. And yes, I could be patient.

And she was correct in that he had to have had previous pain to not be able to let me in. I, personally, thought it was because he lost his friend, Thomas. I couldn't imagine losing Evie. It would be devastating. And it would definitely set me back on my heels for a long time.

I listened to the entire broadcast, trying to absorb the rest of the information about dealing with veterans. I was sure I would forget a lot of it, but if the situation was presented maybe I would remember.

Three hours later, I was trying to remember the Love Vixen's advice to be patient. The podcast was over and he'd had a couple of hours to digest, but I didn't think he was coming.

I was strangely calm as I put the food away, uneaten. I wanted to be the love of his life, but if he wasn't ready, there was no sense in trying to force him. I wanted him to come to me with an open heart, willing to take a chance on us.

I was second-guessing writing the email.

When four hours rolled past, then five, I went to bed. But I didn't cry. In some way I had kind of expected him to disappoint me.

13

I hadn't slept well, and I could feel it. My nerves were quivery, like I could blow up on someone, or something.

The deal to buy the Burle was not going smoothly, and they had added a last minute addendum to the purchase contract before this morning's meeting. I'd read it until the wee hours of the morning, and not been impressed. The owners were basically trying to release themselves from all liability when I took over. In other words, they knew there was some shoddy work or other danger in the building, and they knew I would find it when I did the renovation. I was assuming there was black mold in the walls or something that they hadn't disclosed.

I wasn't going to sign the contract with this clause in it, because the residents deserved more. If they had health issues exacerbated by the conditions they were living in, they needed to have recourse if they wanted to pursue the previous owners.

I was ready to fight.

I showered and dressed and ran the dog, leaving him upstairs when I went to the meeting. I would come back afterward and take a nap, because my eyes were gritty from lost sleep.

Tanner texted me right before I went into the meeting.

So, how was dessert boss man?

What the hell was he talking about?

I replied with a *?* as I ran up the steps to the lawyer's office.

With Catalina! Didn't you go get the dessert?

The sight of Cat's name stalled me out at the top of the stairs, and I moved against the wall. *I don't know what the hell you're talking about.*

The phone rang in my hand. "Dude, seriously? Didn't you listen to the podcast last night?"

"I have to get into a meeting Tanner." I growled. "What are you talking about?"

"Catalina wrote the Love Vixen, and she responded! Dude, you were on the podcast last night, and you were supposed to go eat dinner. Oh, man, Catalina is going to be broken-hearted."

It finally sank in then, what he was telling me, and nausea churned in my gut. Catalina had written the Love Vixen about me? What had the woman said? I glanced at the watch on my wrist. I didn't have time to try to look it up right now. "Can you send me a link to the podcast? I didn't hear it. I'll have to listen to it when I get out of the meeting."

"I'll try to find it. I thought you were listening, now."

I sighed. "I was doing contract work for this meeting last night."

"Ok, I'll try to find the recording."

"Thanks, Tanner."

Catalina broken-hearted, making me dessert. I had more questions than answers, and I needed to focus on this damn deal.

I walked into the conference room and set my briefcase down, looking at the people around the table. My lawyer sat at the head of the table. She'd told me yesterday that they were trying to pass off a bad deal, but I hadn't known how bad. Not until I'd read it myself. The current owners of the building seemed smug, which just cranked my anger. They knew I wanted this building, but I wasn't going to be stupid about getting it.

I dropped the amended contract on the table and shoved it at them. "I'm not signing that. You either drop your price by half or replace the liability clause. If not, I'm out. You can find another buyer."

I sat in the chair, enjoying watching them try to recover. In the end I got my building, and they reluctantly scratched off the addendum part of the contract. My phone buzzed in my pocket, but I waited until I was out of the building before I opened the message. I had a podcast player on my phone, so it connected immediately, routing through the audio system on my truck. I sat there, parked in the street, and listened to the woman read off email after email, then she got to Catalina's.

I could almost hear Cat saying the words. Then there was the invitation to dinner. And dessert. Fuck...

I listened to the Love Vixen's advice twice, then a third time, and the last sentence resonated with me. *Take the chance and follow your heart*. The past eight days without Catalina, without even a glimpse of her, had crippled me. Yeah, I'd stayed up last night looking at that contract, but I hadn't been sleeping well since she'd told me goodbye in the coffee shop. I'd had a few night terrors, mostly about her being attacked and my not being there, then finding her body later. And the anger had dogged my steps constantly.

I was caught in a loop, though. Was the anger spurred on by the fact that I couldn't be with her? And if I returned to her, would the anger ease? I would never want to risk her safety.

I used to dream about losing Thomas and the rest of the men in my team, but it had shifted to Catalina now. The difference was, Thomas was dead, and Catalina was not. So, did I follow my heart like the Love Vixen suggested? It was what I wanted, to be with Cat. It was all I'd wanted the entire time.

I loved her. I knew that. Did I trust myself enough to be with her and hope that my issues wouldn't hurt her? Not really, but I was going to have to try. I was in purgatory right now, and I needed more. I deserved more.

And she didn't deserve to be left like that, wondering. I wish I'd turned on the damned podcast last night, and I could have saved her pain.

I shifted the truck into gear and turned for the Willows.

SOMETHING TOLD me that the knock at the door was Booker, and I debated whether or not to answer it. If he was here to say sorry, it still didn't matter that I loved him, I think I would have to scream in his face. A girl could only be shut down so many times, and I was past my quota for the month.

There was a strong sense of embarrassment, too. I'd basically proclaimed my love for him in front of the how many millions of listeners? As well as my friends and neighbors. Everyone in the building now knew that Booker and I had been a thing. But it was more telling that he was gone. Everyone knew that as well, and now they knew why.

What had I been thinking, writing that woman?

He knocked again. "Catalina. Open the door, please. I know you're home."

I grimaced, knowing I probably looked like shit. I hadn't slept well, and even though I'd showered and scrubbed off all the makeup, I knew I probably looked like a damned witch.

Frowns and anger and sadness made you look old. Or at least I thought it did.

Sighing heavily, I got up from the computer and went to the front door. Might as well get it over with.

I swung the door open and stepped back, allowing him to enter. Oh, damn, he looked incredible. His hair was brushed back and he wore a dark suit jacket over his jeans. The white shirt he wore beneath was open, showing just a hint of chest hair. I turned away, letting him close the door.

"Hey."

"Hey."

"Listen," I told him, moving into the room a little, "you don't have to say anything and make this any more awkward than it already is. Your actions speak louder than words."

"Good," he said, and I realized he was right behind me. Before I could say anything, he cupped my head in his hands and kissed me.

This wasn't an average peck-on-the-lips kind of kiss. No, this was a grinding, wet invasion that fired my senses and made me weak in the knees. When I sagged in his arms, he wrapped one of his around my back to support me as he continued to kiss me. This was unexpected, to say the least, and I scrambled to stay coherent. Yes, he looked good and smelled good and felt amazeballs, but I needed to clarify exactly what was going on. I leaned back against his arm.

"Booker," I breathed, my voice no more than a whisper. "What..."

"I'm sorry. I didn't hear the podcast until an hour ago, when Tanner told me about it."

His voice was even more rough than normal, and I could feel his erection digging into my hip. It was scrambling my brain, and this conversation was too important to get wrong. I pulled back even more.

"I'm sorry, but you've confused me. I think we need to talk."

Booker let me go, and I leaned against the back of the couch.

I wasn't sure my legs would carry me any further. Even weak, though, I wanted to reach out and drag him to me. He looked so incredibly handsome in his suit jacket. "So, what's changed? I mean, you're here, which I appreciate, but I didn't think you were open to more..."

Booker scraped a hand through his hair, making a mess. Frustration tightened his mouth, and he looked down at the floor. He seemed to be counting. "I would never do anything to hurt you," he said finally, bringing his brilliant green gaze up. "But I worry. Before the war, I was pretty calm and level-headed, but the TBI makes me feel things, anger especially, that I normally wouldn't. That first morning after we made love, I woke up so angry I had to leave. And the anger doesn't necessarily have a focus, just boiling emotion in my gut. For the most part, I can drag it back, but sometimes I have to expel it somehow, and I would never want to hurt you."

I looked at him incredulously. "Are you serious? You literally took a knife for me. Do you really think your subconscious mind would ever allow you to hurt me? I don't. No way in hell."

He looked down at the scar on his hand. "I would take a million of these rather than see you hurt."

I reached out to touch his hand. "I believe you. I believe *in* you. I know you think you're this stalwart protector, but there's more to this relationship than that. There has to be balance between us. I love having a protector, I really do, but I want someone to walk by my side, as well. I love that you're talking to me about this, because I would never have known otherwise. It explains why you've been holding back."

His hands cupped mine and when he looked up, his eyes shimmered. "I need to be a part of your life. The past eight days have been hell."

"Agreed," I laughed, tears coming to my own eyes in response to his.

"I need you in my life, Catalina Rivera. I'm tired of going home alone, and sleeping alone. I want more. And I want to give more. I want you to tell me about difficult clients and neat things you've seen. I want to hold you after we make love, and be held by you."

My throat closed up completely then and the tears fell, because I had never experienced a man being so vulnerable. It was humbling, being the one person he could talk to about this.

"I love you, Gabriel Booker," I whispered. "Those eight days were hell for me, too. I wanted to call you up and tell you about my boring day, and fall asleep talking to you on the phone. I just want to hear you breathe and watch you walk and moan as you eat my food. I want to see you puff up your chest when you're protecting me. Most especially, though, I want you to look at me like that." I motioned to his eyes, and they softened as he smiled. "You may not be ready to say the words yet, but I can see you love me in everything you do."

Without a word he pulled me into his arms, wrapping me so tight it was hard to breathe. Then, surprising me even more, he swung me up into his arms. I laughed, because he was the only man that had ever dared do this, and I loved it. I trusted him completely, and I knew where we were going.

Kicking the door shut, he maneuvered so that I could lock the deadbolts, then he turned down the hallway. The man wasn't even breathing hard when he dropped me to the bed, then followed me down. He tossed his suit jacket aside and started on the buttons of the shirt. I batted his hands away and got them done faster, spreading the shirt wide. Rounded pecs strained as he held himself over me, and there were veins visible down the length of his arms. How fucking sexy was that?

No, what was even more sexy was the look on his face. Gabriel Booker was always drool-worthy, but horny and anticipating a good lay? Yeah, he was even more striking, his gaze focused directly on me. "I want that shirt off."

I thought he was talking about his own for a minute, but no, he had focused on my breasts. Shimmying beneath him, I twisted the shirt up over my head and tossed it away. He leaned back enough to leer down at me and toss his own shirt away, then to kick off his pants and shoes. My mouth watered as I caught sight of his straining erection in the maroon athletic underwear, the head of him up his belly. I wanted to ride that man.

"Lay down," I told him. For a moment he didn't do anything, then he flopped over onto his back, presenting me with six feet and a few inches of mouth-watering former Army Ranger. I let him lay there as I stepped to the side of the bed and stripped down, very, very slowly. The bra went first, then I skimmed the black leggings down my thighs, and down my calves, kicking them away. The panties were a bare scrap of lace, and they dropped to the floor. When I looked back at him, he'd rolled onto his side to watch me and was holding his erection in his hand, lightly jacking the shaft.

My body was drenched with need for him, and seeing him that way, just as needy, was heady. Moving to the bed, I tipped him back onto his back and straddled his hips. I giggled as he lifted us both up and to the center of the mattress. We'd been a little close to the edge.

Those strong hands held my hips, though, not letting me take him in. "I just want to watch you go down slow," he whispered. Reaching between our bodies, I shoved his underwear out of the way and stood his penis up, then Booker began to lower me. He glided in and filled me up like I had literally been built to accommodate him. It was sublime, and sent a rush of heat up through my body, all the way out to my fingertips. I sat up straight and he went even deeper, then he reached up to cup my breasts. "You have a shape built for loving," he told me, and he started to move.

My body contracted as he withdrew, as if to hold him in, then relaxed as I glided down. "Oh," I sighed as I settled into a rhythm. This was such a different feeling from being on the bottom, and I loved it. I swiveled my hips, looking for the sweet spot, and I found it. I glided over and over that spot, building momentum, and I could tell he was nearing that peak as well. He felt so damn good...

I was a little confused when he pulled me down toward him, and I thought he wanted me to kiss him, so I did, but then he began to piston his hips up into me, fast, and the dynamic changed drastically. I thought I was in control, but he totally just overwhelmed me. It was glorious. That stream that had been building changed into a river of sensation, and before I could voice a protest the orgasm had slammed into me. I braced with my head buried in his neck as wave after wave of release flowed over me. His strong arms wrapped around my body and I heard him whispering into my hair.

Booker didn't give me a chance to catch my breath. Levering over, he took the power position, keeping our bodies together as he did it. Then he lifted my knees and spread me wide, surging deep. "The feel of you coming as you grip my dick is breathtaking, Cat, and I want more."

His hips drew back, then slid deep, and he built his own rhythm. It was his turn to drive the bus, so to speak, and he drove it hard. The orgasm that had been fading began to build again. And when his orgasm hit and made him cry out, I was right there with him, my body seemingly on a different, pleasure-soaked plane of existence. My body just kept spasming with his as we fed off each other. It was something I'd never experienced before with any other man.

It took a while for our bodies to recover. Booker pulled a

sheet over top of us and pulled me into his arms, and I think we slept for a while. Then we roused and he flipped me over onto my belly, gliding into me from behind. My sensitive body responded to the new position with a flood of moisture, and Booker ground himself into me, panting. "You are incredible, Cat. I can't get enough of you."

"Good," I told him firmly, arching my hips up into his plunge, "because I think this is my new favorite position,." I said as fresh pleasure shot through me like heat lightning. My release triggered his own, and I pushed my hips up so that he could get a tiny bit deeper.

His raspy voice broke as he found his release, and I felt a surge of love in my heart so clear, it brought tears to my eyes. "I love you, Gabriel."

"I love you, babe."

I caught my breath, but he didn't even seem to notice what he'd said. His body was demanding his attention as it played out its pleasure, and when it was done, he lowered himself to my back. A kiss whispered in near my ear. "I think you've officially wrung me dry."

I laughed and curled one of his hands beneath me. "I doubt that. We'll get a shower and some food, and you'll be ready to go again."

"You're probably right."

"I'm not going to get any work done, today," I laughed.

I COULD LITERALLY FEEL the satisfaction ease the knot of anger that had been living in my gut for the past week. Curly, dark hair was tickling my neck, my prosthetic was dislodging and my ass was cold to the air, but none of it mattered because I had

Catalina in my arms. After we'd caught our breath, we'd walked to the shower hand in hand.

As she adjusted the taps, I removed my prosthetic. She had a walk-in shower, which was nice, but if there was any soap on the floor at all my leg would slip out beneath me as I hopped in. Luckily, I didn't disgrace myself this time, and I lowered myself to the bench in the back. Cat unmounted the shower head and held it in her hands, focused on herself, so that it wouldn't blast me.

I reached out and cupped her hips in my hands, pulling her down to sit on my good knee. She wrapped an arm around my shoulders and directed the water to shower down on our shoulders, making it run down our backs and fronts. "Thank you for today," I told her.

She made a face. "I don't think thanks are necessary. I love you. I'm in love with you. Nothing I give or do for you costs."

I teased a dark tan nipple, and even in the heat it tightened. They both did. Running my hand down her belly, I teased at her folds, cupping and guiding the water there. She was so swollen, and slick from her releases and my own. I rubbed very carefully, rinsing her clean, then I took the head of the shower from her. Turning the dial, I backed off the pressure of the stream, and guided it down her body. She gasped as it hit her sensitive flesh, but seemed to enjoy it as well. Her head tipped back on my shoulder and her knees spread wide, so I directed the stream in tiny circles. She gasped and writhed against me.

"A little harder," she said, and I adjusted the water pressure, then went back to circling her clit. Within seconds she gave a cry and her body rippled with release. It didn't slam into her like it did before, but washed over her in gentle undulations. It was sexy as fuck. She covered herself with a hand and I moved the water away. I pressed a kiss to the side of her face. "Are you okay?"

Cat nodded, saying nothing. It took her a solid minute to open her eyes and look at me. "I don't think I can give any more today," she chuckled.

I grinned at her, taking that as a challenge. We'd see how she felt tonight.

"Do you have any leftovers from that dinner?"

Cocking a brow at me, she smiled, lopsided. "Maybe..."

After we washed each other down, we went to the kitchen to scour the fridge. Cat brought out container after container of food, and started dishing out portions on plates. Once it was warm, we sat at the counter and ate, our knees resting against each other.

"I wish I had been here to eat this when you first made it," I murmured, swallowing down the last of my water. "I'm sorry I wasn't."

Cat shrugged, but I could see the pain in her eyes.

"I will never intentionally hurt you," I said firmly, "but that being said, I know I'm going to fumble. If I do something wrong, let me know so I can fix it and understand, okay?"

She nodded, a gentle smile on her lips. "I will instruct you in all things."

"Good," I said, smiling, looking forward to the adventure.

EPILOGUE

I loved the bench Booker had added to the laundry room. It was just tall enough for me to lean in and reach the bottom of the drum, gathering all of my, our, things. Some of these were Booker's underwear and shirts.

I didn't mind doing his laundry, and I absolutely loved cooking him dinner. It was part of our ritual, now. On the days he had to be out of the building, I made sure to welcome him home with a kiss. Sometimes it developed into more and sometimes it didn't, but either way we were always happy to see one another.

I kept waiting for that to change, but I literally looked forward to seeing him every moment I could. We had just passed the three months mark in our relationship, and the thrill that went through me when I heard him coming down the hallway was just as strong now as it was when we first got together.

The Burle was under renovation now, and it was taking a lot of energy. When he came home, dirty and tired, there was a new satisfaction to his demeanor. The Burle housed a bunch of veterans, and I knew he was really enjoying getting to know them. It took a lot of time, though.

I heard the key in the lock and I tossed the dish towel aside to walk out to the living room. I got to the door just as it swung open, and I walked straight into his arms. Blue danced around our legs, happy to be home as well. The dog went with him most days.

Booker wrapped his arms around me and lifted my feet off the ground so he could stand straight. "Hi, babe. I missed you."

"I missed you too, sexy. How are the guys?"

"They're fine. I think Tanner's in love again. One of the vets has a granddaughter who comes out to take him to appointments and stuff. Anyway, Tanner has been dating her for the past week."

I laughed as he set me down. "A whole week. Wow..."

Booker shrugged. "It's something that it's more than a one-night stand."

"True."

Poor Tanner.

"In other news," I said, switching gears. "Dinner will be a celebration."

Booker paused and looked at me. "Did he plead?"

I nodded.

For four months the threat of having to go to court and testify about Sean and Lincoln's attack had dogged me. I didn't want to talk about Sean any more. My life was so different, now. I had Booker and Blue, and Evie was coming back to the states in a month. It was time to move on. "Seven years total, and Lincoln pled out to three. Not as much as I wanted, but better than nothing. My lawyer said their lawyer was an idiot and had fumbled a few things, so that helped as well."

Booker snorted. "That's what you get when your family doesn't fork out cash for the best lawyers in town."

"Yes. Jeffrey stuck to his word. I'm sure it was hard on him and I thought about sending him a note or something."

Booker grinned at me, shaking his head. "Only you would do that. I love you, babe. You have a wonderful heart."

I walked into his arms and leaned against his chest. My fingers went to the belt loops at his hips and rested there, and he wrapped his arms around my neck. This was my safe place, wrapped in his arms, with the dog leaning against us both. "Well," he rumbled beneath my chest, "I had a feeling they would plead out and we would have a good night, so, I might have gotten you something."

Leaving me standing near the couch, he returned to the apartment door and opened it. "Blue, go get the bag."

Blue shot through the door and disappeared down the hallway. I laughed, wondering what he'd taught him now. Last week Booker had taught the dog to carry a bunch of flowers to me, and the week before that he'd jumped on the bed with a stuffed squishy octopus thing. That one might have been chewed a little bit on one of the legs, but he'd given it up to me, his short little nubbin tail wiggling.

I grinned as I watched him lunge through the door, the handles of a pretty pink bag in his mouth. I took the bag and rubbed his head. "Thank you, Blue."

It was stuffed with pink tissue paper. I pulled them out one by one and dropped them to the floor, until I got to a box. It was small and square. I set the bag on the floor amidst the paper, and opened the box, my heart picking up speed. Inside was what appeared to be a ring box.

I glanced up at Booker, but he was frowning. He nodded his chin at me to keep going, so I dumped the jewelry box out of the little square box. Then I flipped open the lid, not daring to breathe.

"Oh," I breathed, tears flooding my eyes.

The ring was perfection. With a beautiful cushion cut diamond in the center of the scrolling platinum setting, it was flanked by little emeralds around the center piece and along the band.

We'd been walking along the street one evening after we'd had dinner, and there'd been a jewelry store. The emeralds had caught my eye, and apparently his as well. This wasn't the same ring I'd seen. This one was more beautiful. I lifted my gaze in time to see him go down on his good knee. He took the ring from me and set the box aside.

"Catalina, you've taught me so much over the past few months. More than I ever could have imagined. You've given me a home and a place to be safe with what I feel."

The tears were rolling down my cheeks now, but there was no way I could stop them. He was kneeling in front of me, the ring held up to me, and there was a sweet quiver in his raspy voice.

"I worried that I would feel trapped in a relationship, but you've made me a willing captive. I want to be yours for the rest of my life. I love you, Catalina. Will you marry me?"

I cried as I nodded. "Yes, five million times, yes!"

That had taken a lot for him to say, and I was so full of emotion. It had been a harrowing day, waiting to hear if the brothers pled out, but it was going to end on a high note. Maybe the highest note I'd ever been a part of.

His hands shaking, Booker slid the ring onto my ring finger. I had no idea how he'd known my size, but it fit perfectly. "Oh, Gabriel, it's stunning."

After the ring was seated, he kissed my finger, as if to seal it on. Then he stood to take me into his arms. His mouth covered mine in a gentle kiss, and I knew I'd found my unreachable dream. I pulled back, grinning, wiping the tears from my face. "Hey, now I'm really your fiancée."

Booker chuckled. "You know, I think my mind recognized that you were the one for me, and that's why it popped out of my mouth so easily that night."

"Probably," I agreed. "We need to write the Love Vixen with an update."

Booker rolled his eyes, laughing. "Oh, hell... If you had any idea of the ribbing I got from the guys last time for screwing that up..."

I laughed, because even though he groused about it, it had been the most important night of our lives. Well, maybe the second most important now.

"I'm going to write her," I grinned. "I love you, Gabriel."

"I love you, Catalina."

He cupped my head in his hands and kissed me. And we didn't have dinner for a very long time.

"*Okay, listeners*," the Love Vixen said at the beginning of the Friday podcast, her voice full of satisfaction, "*I received a note this week that makes my job so rewarding. A few months ago Desperate in Columbus wrote me about a struggle she was having with her hunky building manager slash former Army Ranger in shining armor, Booker. He'd rescued her from a dangerous situation, then ghosted on her. She'd invited him to dinner, knowing that he listened to the show, with dessert after.*

"*Well, he apparently came for dessert and stayed, because I'm looking at a picture of a gorgeous engagement ring. Congratulations go out to Booker and Catalina! May you live a long, happy life.*"

THE END...

THE LOVE VIXEN

***Disclaimer. The Love Vixen is a fictional character. She is not a doctor and her advice should probably never be followed. Anything resembling an actual event or article is completely ridiculous because I made the whole thing up!

Ready for More Love Vixen Books?

If this is your first Love Vixen book,

check out the entire series here: The Love Vixen.

Wouldn't you like to be a Vixen too?

Join our private and interactive Facebook Group or Party Central as we like to call it: **https://www.facebook.com/ groups/TheLoveVixN**

Don't miss any of the Love Vixen's year of release celebrations!

Sign up for The Love Vixen Newsletter: https:// bit.ly/TheLoveVixen

Next up!!!
Bone Frog Love by Sharon Hamilton
Dear Love Vixen:

I'm flirting with this guy who is almost as old as my dad. I mean, he's hot as hell, and he's a real man, not like the boys I've been dating lately. Is this wrong? I know, I know. I need to find out if he's married, or with someone first, but he wants to take me out on a lunch date to discuss. Should I go, or nip it in the bud? I can't stop thinking/dreaming about him.

Cupcake Girl:

Nip it. Nip it. Nip it. Until you know what you're dealing with don't get your heart involved. Don't listen to those naughty girly parts until you know he's single and available. And by available, I also mean emotionally. Then decide what you want from him and what's best for you. Which may or may not be the same thing.

Good luck, hon. XOXO LV

Thoughts From An Older Man:

"From the first moment I saw her I envisioned slapping frosting all over that cute little cupcake at the Baby Cakes bar. When I close my eyes I'm dribbling warm chocolate sauce, powdered sugar, silver balls and sprinkles all over her body parts and then...OMG I shouldn't be even considering dating someone so young. But I'm newly single now and this sweet young thing seems like just the right person I could take another bite out of love with. I've weathered the marriage storms and served my country well for twenty years. Isn't a former Navy SEAL allowed a little fun?"

Amazon-
    Amazon UK-
    Amazon CA-
    Amazon AU-

ABOUT THE AUTHOR

NY Times and USA Today Bestselling author J.M. Madden writes compelling romances between 'combat modified' military men and the women who love them. J.M. Madden loves any and all good love stories, most particularly her own. She has two beautiful children and a husband who always keeps her on her toes.

J.M. was a Deputy Sheriff in Ohio for nine years, until hubby moved the clan to Kentucky. When not chasing the family around, she's at the computer, reading and writing, perfecting her craft. She occasionally takes breaks to feed her animal horde and is trying to control her office-supply addiction, but both tasks are uphill battles. Happily, she is writing full-time and always has several projects in the works. She also dearly loves to hear from readers! So, drop her a line. She'll respond.

My Facebook LIKE Page- https://www.facebook.com/JMMadden58

✔Follow me on Twitter-- @authorjmmadden

✔Sign up for my Newsletter if you haven't already. You get 4 free books!

✔Follow me on Instagram--

The Lost and Found Series Discussion Group-https://www.facebook.com/groups/433871413415527

OR you can email me at authorjmmadden@gmail.com

ALSO-

If you love the book, **PLEASE** leave a review! We really do notice a difference when readers support us!

Thank you so much!

JM

ALSO BY JM MADDEN

When you sign up for my newsletter on my website, you receive 4 free books, the beginnings to three series. Go to jmmadden.com and sign up!

If you would like to read about the 'combat modified' veterans of the **Lost and Found Investigative Service**, check out these books:

The Embattled Road

Duncan, John and Chad

Embattled Hearts-Book 1

John and Shannon

Embattled Minds-Book 2

Zeke and Ember

Embattled Home-Book 3

Chad and Lora

Embattled SEAL- Book 4

Harper and Cat

Embattled Ever After- Book 5

Duncan and Alex

Her Forever Hero- Grif

Grif and Kendall

SEAL's Lost Dream-Flynn

Flynn and Willow

SEAL's Christmas Dream

Flynn and Willow

Unbreakable SEAL-

Max and Lacey

Embattled Christmas

Reclaiming The Seal

Gabe and Julie

Loving Lilly

Diego and Lilly

Her Secret Wish

Rachel and Dean

Wish Upon a SEAL

Drake and Izzy

Mistletoe Mischief

Cass and Roger

Lost and Found Pieces

Lost and Found Pieces 2

There are two Lost and Found Spinoff series, the Lowells and the Dogs of War, which heads in a bit of a paranormal direction.

The Lowells of Honeywell, Texas Box Set

Forget Me Not

Untying his Not

Naughty by Nature

Trying the Knot

The Dogs of War

Genesis

Chaos

Destruction

Retribution

Catalyst

If you love dogs and would like to read about a concierge service helping military personnel out of difficult spots, check out:

Healing Home

Wicked Healing

Healing Hope (Coming Soon!)

If you would like to read a Navy SEAL book with more mature characters, check out

SEAL Hard

Flat Line

Other books by J.M. Madden

A Touch of Fae

Second Time Around

A Needful Heart

Wet Dream

Love on the Line

The Billionaire's Secret Obsession

Made in the USA
Coppell, TX
24 August 2021

61088908R00104